FAITHLESS ROMANCE
BY
PATRICIA SHANNON
AND
YOGESH BHATT

First Edition
Copyright
Patricia Shannon & Yogesh Bhatt
2017

Chapter 1

Claire flinched and clenched her hands around the armrests. The plane entered another area of turbulence and shuddered again. She enjoyed an occasional thrill, but this time the constant trembling further rattled her aggravated nerves.
The blonde, broad-shouldered man sitting next to her seemed oblivious to her inner struggle. In stark contrast to herself, he appeared relaxed, listening to music through the headphones. He sipped at a glass of red wine, served by the stewardess, only minutes ago.
Distraught, she tried to divert her attention to the articles in the in-flight magazine. Her forthcoming new life down under with Nathan excited her. Yet the thought of whom she left behind, saddened her. Tears welled up. The words on the pages in front of her blurred by her watery eyes.
Once again, she doubted her own judgment. She questioned her decision to join Nathan on his quest for adventure. Not convinced her desire for pleasures warranted the risk she took.
She never intended to hurt Mason, but it happened. Even though he gave her everything that a woman could want, she became bored by the lack of excitement. It suffocated her. And despite the fact that she loved him, she needed to break away from the comfort and the security. She grabbed every opportunity that came her way.
When Nathan persisted in his court-making, he took their work relationship to a whole different level.
He succeeded to win her over for an intoxicating affair.

She tried to keep the best of both. A perfect combination of safety with a touch of danger, pleasure, and excitement. But, she underestimated Mason's sixth sense, and he caught her in the act. Leaving her to face the unfortunate consequences of her mistake. The way he confronted her and ended their betrothal almost seemed paradoxical.
The sound of Nathan's voice startled her.
"Is everything alright?" he asked concerned, meanwhile caressing the side of her face with his bronzed hand. "You look awfully distressed."
She loosened the muscles in her neck.
"Yes and no," she replied with a gentle smile. "I'm looking forward to our new life together. And yet, I think about Mason. In a way, I feel sorry for him. It must be so hard on him right now." She sighed.
He took the plugs out of his ears and responded discerned. "That's understandable, breaking up is never easy." He looked at her, now more serious.
"Although I warned you about him! I hope you're not having any second thoughts?"
"No, no," she was quick to deny. "Don't worry, I haven't. It's just that he didn't deserve it, that's all."
"Well, no-one deserves it, to be honest," he said, annoyed. "But you made a decision. We are now moving on. I'm sure he will as well. He's a grown man. He can take care of himself."
Claire realized it was better to change the topic.
It became clear Nathan left that part of their life behind him. He wished to focus on their new beginning.

Faithless Romance

"Of course, he will get over it!" she replied, submissive, trying to avoid having an argument in mid-air. "Once he meets someone new, he will forget me!"

She watched another passenger, walking up and down the isle. The thought of Mason with someone else only added to her anxiety.

Confused and tired, she laid her head on Nathan's shoulder. She attempted to push her musing over the past to the background.

He put a comforting arm around her waist and gave her a soft kiss on the cheek. The closeness of his firm and warm body soon calmed her down. His affection reassured her.

She decided to accept the change, with more faith.

"I can't wait to see our new apartment," she spoke optimistic. "From what I've seen in the pictures, the view from the balcony is incredible! You won't find that anywhere in London!" she acknowledged.

"Yes, you'll like it," he said pleased. "It's amazing! Spacious and bright!" he boasted. "And you will love the area of Sydney's Bondi Beach! It buzzes with activity; cafe's, bars, lots of shops and there's plenty of entertainment. They organize a range of events each year. It's a great place to be!"

"I take your word for it," she responded consoled and yawning. "I think I'll try to sleep. It's still a long way to go, and I'm exhausted. I want to have energy left once we land over there."

"Sounds like a good idea," he answered.

"I follow your lead."

They pushed their chairs backward and closed their eyes.

But, Claire tried in vain to get the rest she wanted.
She couldn't find a comfortable position to lay her head or her long legs. Not to mention the noises on the crowded plane. People chatted away, babies cried, and the crew came around with food and drinks on a regular basis.
On top of that, the frequent bumps in the sky kept her on edge and unsettled.
Unable to stay sound asleep, her thoughts wandered back again to the life she left behind. The day she first set eyes on Mason when they collided in the middle of a footpath. Still vivid in her mind.

Chapter 2

Upset and restless, Claire looked everywhere. On the pavement, in corners, and underneath rubbish.
"Please let me find it!" she muttered. "This can't be happening! I'm running late for work! It must be here, somewhere!" She became stressed and desperate.
Engrossed in her search, she never noticed the man in front of her until their bodies collided. The impact brought her to an abrupt standstill.
"Oh, my goodness!" she cried out. "I'm so sorry!"
In an instant, the stranger put his protective arms around her. And for a moment, they stood in an embrace together. His body felt firm and comforting. A powerful scent of cinnamon mixed with sandalwood entered her nostrils. She further inhaled the captivating aroma, and she relished its calming and soothing effect.
"No need to apologize!" he responded. His voice sounded gentle. "Are you all right?" he then asked, concerned. "You looked rather tense."
Embarrassed, she forced herself to snap out of the enchanting spell. She shook off her amorous thoughts and looked straight into his sparkling, enthralling eyes.
"Yes, I'm fine, thank you!" she said. "And you? I hope I didn't hurt you?"
"No, not at all!" he answered with a smile. "I consider myself the luckiest man on Earth right now!"
At first glance, his demeanor disappointed her.
She imagined a different man wearing such an exquisite aftershave.

And yet, an incomprehensible power radiated out from him. He appeared confident in his well-fitted navy blue suit. His steady gaze with his intense dark brown eyes dazzled her. She could hear her heart pounding faster and held her breath, wondering if he noticed. For an inexplicable reason, his whole presence overwhelmed and confused her. Unlike plenty of other men.

He kept looking at her with an amused smile on his face.

"Can I help you?" he went on. "You searched for something?"

She gazed back at him. Not sure whether to accept his aid or not. I can't say there's a physical attraction. He's not that handsome. But still, he knocked me over!

She grinned. It puzzled her.

"Sorry," she hastened to say. "I lost a valuable gold bracelet I wore on my wrist. My late mother gave it for my 18th birthday. I have to find it! I think it came loose right there!" She pointed at a spot back down the road.

"I'll be heartbroken if the wristlet is gone forever!" She became emotional about the loss of her mother's heirloom. At once he responded to her despair, with a sympathetic smile.

"Let me join you in your search!" he said. "Being a jeweler myself, I know such a lovely present is precious.

And, by the way, my name is Mason, Mason Brannigan. I'm the owner of that store over there!" He pointed at a well-presented boutique shop across the road from London's Oxford Street.

She saw the name *'Brannigan's Jewelry Emporium'* on a signboard above the store window.

Written in gold leaf letters.

What a coincidence that he owns a jewelry store! she thought. He could be a prospective client for the firm. An appealing prospect. "Nice to meet you too!" she responded cheerfully.

"My name is Claire, Claire Attaway!"

"Claire!" He repeated her name with a twinkle in his eyes. "Can you describe the gift to me? It's better we search now before the shopping crowd arrives. Or you may indeed lose it forever!"

"Yes, of course, you're right," she said. "It's a gold ringlet bracelet encrusted with small diamonds." She began searching again.

Mason's eyes wandered over the path. He saw a small pile of rubbish at the edge of the footpath. The perfect hiding place for a small item. And, within minutes, he caught sight of the lost heirloom.

"Look what I found!" he called out.

When she rushed towards him, their bodies came together and she savored his warmth, flustered and entranced.

"Thank you, oh thank you!" she said, rejoiced. She secured the bracelet around her wrist, gloating from relief and gratitude.

"Can I repay you with dinner tonight?" she asked him.

"It will be my pleasure to share an evening with a lovely lady!" he replied, charmed by her invitation.

"But, if you'll excuse me, I have to open my shop! Please come in, and let me write down your phone number."

"Sure!" she answered, flattered by his earlier remark, although men always complimented her.

"But I'm already late for work, so I have to make it short!" They meanwhile crossed the road together.

How lucky to meet such a great potential client! Whether he bumped into me on purpose or not, she thought. The best excuse to use on my boss for my late arrival!

She liked a new challenge, in business or on a more personal level. The possibility to win him over for the firm that evening exhilarated her. But she also wanted to learn more about the man behind the surface.

When she walked into the shop, the interior impressed her. "What a great presentation of your collection!" she commented. "The mahogany counter and those wall boards! Truly amazing!" She rattled on.

"The sparkling gold and the diamonds will attract many women to your shop, I guess. You must have a lot of girlfriends?" she asked, with a bold and defiant expression on her face.

He remained silent at first. Her forwardness took him by surprise. She flirted with him. But she also impressed and fascinated him.

"To answer your question," he replied at last. "I have no girlfriend!"

She stared back at him, thinking there could be another opportunity. "You are joking, right?" she provoked him.

"No, trust me, I'm not! I've met no one suitable yet! Until now, that is." He shied her with an intense gaze.

"And how is your business?" she hurried to say. "I'm a Management Consultant you see.

Available to offer you a few recommendations, to help you further expand your enterprise."

She tried to warm him up for their meeting that evening. Though somehow he appeared annoyed with her suggestion.

But her remarks dumbfounded Mason. Not only because he met a most elegant woman by chance. She manifested shrewdness and professionalism. He liked and wanted her even more. But he figured that he needed to take it slow. So he stayed calm and composed.

"Let's talk it over tonight," she dared him, trying to gain momentum. "I have to dash off now, or my boss will kill me! Remember! Seven pm at Charlie's!"

She smiled her most ravishing smile and left him unable to think of an excuse.

She remained awestruck by this unexpected event. Special thoughts and new found feelings arose in her. It didn't make sense.

I meet plenty of men, most of them successful and far more interesting, she reflected. Always with a strong sexual attractiveness and a slight, superficial affection. Then why is it different this time? Why do I feel drawn to him? What's his secret?

Chapter 3

Claire worked for the well-known, multinational company, Baxter Corporate Management. The building, showcasing a blue glass facade, stood on Wells Street, a side street of Oxford Street. A part of the city called Westminster. An area with a mixture of old and new. Close to the University, with modern and historic buildings, restaurants and shops. It buzzed with activity.
You could not speak of any serious activity in Claire's office, though. She found it difficult to concentrate on her work during the rest of the day. Time appeared to stand still and the day dragged on. At last, it turned six pm, to get dressed for her date with her soon-to-be client.
Once home, she took a quick shower. When she finished, she stood deliberating for a while in front of her clothes. She ended up wearing a soft green cocktail dress.
Her shiny, long auburn hair tightened up, and strings curled around her lovely almond colored face. A gold rope chain necklace and matching earrings complemented her outfit. And, she wore the bracelet. She'd never go without it. Pleased with her looks for the evening, she smiled at her reflection in the mirror.
She grabbed the keys to her black Volkswagen Golf and began the 15-minute drive to Charlie's. A well-known restaurant in London town, popular with business people and jet-set alike.
It provided a warm cozy atmosphere, great food, and friendly waiting staff. Claire showcased a cultivated taste that many friends admired her for.

Faithless Romance

When she arrived, the head waiter escorted her to the candlelit table for two. She reserved it herself during the day and asked for a private corner in the room. To her surprise, Mason sat waiting for her.

He looked stunning in his black cotton dress pants and a soft yellow silk shirt. Despite his ordinary facial looks! His raven black hair combed backward in straight lines.

"There you are!" she greeted him with a happy voice. "I'm glad you're here!"

"So am I!" he replied in an indistinct tone.

He stood up and to her delight, he kissed her on the cheek. She touched the spot on her face with her hand and she still felt the heat of his lips when she sat down at the table. When they looked over the menu to order their meal, she peeked over the edge of the card, trying to read his face. His stern and tense look gave her the impression he tried to hide his emotions.

"I better begin a conversation on personal matters," she thought. "His reaction earlier today about his business makes it somewhat difficult to start with."

When the waiter finished taking their order, she tried a casual remark. "Isn't this a great place to have dinner?" she said. "I looked forward to our meal together tonight," she confessed.

"Yes, it's lovely," he replied. "A good choice!" He looked around. "I've been here before. The food is fantastic!"

"I know," she responded, content. "That's why I chose it! I often eat here with colleagues and friends."

But she noticed his hesitation to take matters more personal.

"Well, at least, I tried," she thought. "But what's the deal with this guy? First, he runs into me on purpose and then he plays it cool?" She doubted her own intuition.

"Perhaps I should talk about business," she supposed. Only to get disappointed about his reserved response to her marketing proposals. Unlike other men in her circles, who were more agreeable towards her. Besides, she knew she was one of the best in her field.

Mason took a casual sip of his wine and tried to keep his act together. He pretended to be confident and distant. But deep inside the pandemonium broke loose. The moment he laid eyes on her, she fascinated him. A sexy, good-looking intelligent woman. Now sitting across from him.

"Why does a woman of her allure show such an interest in me?" he wondered. "I know she tries to win me over for a contract. But, then why the signals to lure me in playing an amorous game? It's obvious she's flirting with me. The way she flicks her hair when she speaks. How she licks her full sensual lips with her tongue. And the gentle touches of her hands when she explains something to me."

He decided that for now, it would be best to keep his cool, no matter how strenuous.

Claire became restless, curious about what went on inside his head.

What does he want from me? Any other man would have made a move by now. Is he determined to make me work for it? She thought she knew what each man wanted from her, but not this time. Well, I'm not going to let him spoil my evening!

She persisted in tantalizing him.

They continued their chitchat about living in London, their spare time and general interests.

It became more and more difficult for Mason to stay level-headed. During their meal, their conversation became more pleasant and interesting. An hour later, the ice broke.

I can't deny her marketing skills and experience in that field, he admitted to himself. She's amazing! Even though he still held back, she won him over.

"May I offer you my business support over the next few months?" she asked.

"Yes!" he replied, thrilled. "I will accept your offer. It sounds good!" He took another sip of his wine.

Claire watched him with intense interest for a while, still under his spell. He impressed her. The more she watched him and the more she listened to what he had to say, the more she liked him. She realized he didn't fall all over her, the way other men used to do.

For that reason, she fantasized that she found a potential husband. She convinced herself she wouldn't have to compete with other women.

Several times before, someone else beat her to it, and her dream prince slipped away. But she doubted whether she could handle a marriage.

When they finished their after-dinner coffee, he snapped her back to reality. The question came on the spur of the moment.

"Would you like to go for a short walk? It's a lovely evening and we can stroll along the waterfront for a while."

Faithless Romance

"What a wonderful idea! Yes, thank you!" she replied, delighted that he wished to spend more time with her.

They walked alongside the bank of the river Thames. The clear sky displayed an exuberant number of stars, flickering above their heads. In the near distance, a view of the glimmering city lights.

What a perfect romantic evening, she thought. Why is Mason so out of reach? He's such a mystery! Is that what makes him attractive?

She wished he'd take her by the hand or put his arms around her, but he didn't. Silence fell between them. A comfortable stillness, she hoped. Not because they had nothing more in common. She tried to stay inconspicuous as she glanced at him.

Still, Mason sensed it. Inflamed with uncontrollable lust, he turned his body towards hers.

"Isn't this amazing?" he said. "We are in the middle of town yet everything seems so peaceful, so calm."

She smiled at him with her most radiant smile. The look in her eyes made him melt on the spot.

"Yes, it is a beautiful evening! I'm so happy to share it with you!" she whispered.

His facial expression softened, and he came closer. He put an arm around her waist. She didn't pull back.

Again, she felt the heat of his skin. The amazing fragrance of his aftershave still lingered around him. It drifted along her nostrils and acted as an aphrodisiac.

As if by magic, he overcame his apprehensions and his lips covered hers in a long warm kiss. He groaned and pulled her closer. His embrace became more demanding.

She didn't resist. Instead, she satisfied his hunger for passion.

They stood right underneath a large sycamore tree. His whole body responded and so did hers. It was the most intense moment she'd ever experienced in her entire life.

When their lips parted, she gazed at him, lost for words. Neither of them spoke. They returned to their cars, arms entwined.

"I can't wait to get together again," he confessed to her. "Do you have time to come over to my place tomorrow? I'll make us a special meal and we can go over more business ideas?"

"That sounds great!" she replied, and she placed a soft kiss on his mouth. He responded with eagerness, and again, they surrendered to the passion for each other.

"Make it around seven?" he broke the spell.

"Yes," she replied, still dazed by her own strong desires towards him, "that's fine."

"Oh, I almost forgot," he said, with a naughty grin on his face, "do you still have your bracelet?"

She grabbed her wrist right away, only to find it there. "You tricked me!" she replied and giggled.

"You better get used to it!" he joked before he stepped into his white Ford Focus.

She watched him drive off into the night. Back in her own car, she listened to her favorite music, love songs by Maria Carey. She arrived home in the happiest mood she ever had. Gleeful for breaking Mason's resistance. And looking forward to continuing their new found affection.

But, things didn't turn out as she expected.

Chapter 4

The rest became a blur when at last, Claire fell asleep on the plane, until she woke up to find the cabin lights switched on and the crew serving breakfast. That meant they arrived in Sydney in three hours from now. She looked around, dazed and slumberous. She yawned and stretched her legs.

"Hello sleepy head," Nathan spoke for the first time in hours. "You were far away in dreamland!"

She yawned again and smiled at him with affection. "Yes, I was," she said, "far, far away!"

She ate the small meal.

An omelet with sausages, a bun, yogurt, and fruit. She stared in front of her, not ready to do any more talking.

When she finished her coffee, her eyelids became heavy and this time, she slept tight. She didn't wake up until Nathan pinched her in the arm. He told her that the plane had landed and that they were to disembark.

They spent an hour getting through immigration and collecting their luggage. They then picked up their hired car to drive to their new home.

In November, the weather is warm and pleasant. They opted for a mini cooper convertible car to drive around during the first week.

Claire looked forward to going sightseeing. This was the real life! A handsome, outgoing boyfriend, a classy car, and apartment. And, the prospect of working together at the Sydney-based office of their UK employer!

A wonderful opportunity!

Any person would be mad not to accept such an awesome deal. But in the back of her mind, she kept on reminiscing. She hoped over time, the memory of Mason would fade away.

She admired the scenery of the large city during their drive to Bondi. Many modern high rise buildings interspersed with historic houses and landmarks. The streets lined with palm trees and exotic birds gathered near fountains and in parks. She could enjoy living here, that much was certain.

Nathan first drove passed the beach itself, before heading towards their apartment buildings. It looked crowded and here and there, buskers provided the public with entertainment.

"This is fantastic!" she commented. "Like you said, such a vibrant area!"

"I knew you'd appreciate it," he replied, smiling at her.

She combed through her lush hair with her fingers and then did the same to his. The intimate moment strengthened her.

"There it is!" Nathan announced, "our new City Hub!"

He pointed at a ten-story high building with lots of glass and a tropical garden in front of it. They drove through a gate into a garage underneath. Just before they went underground, she spotted a swimming pool on the side of the building.

"There's a pool?" she asked, surprised.

"Yes, there is!" he said. "Didn't I mention that? There's also a fitness room."

"Wow!" she responded, excited.

"That's super! How luxurious!"

"We deserve the luxury," he concluded, "we work hard for it."

"That's true," she admitted.

They got their luggage out of the car booth and took the lift to the eighth floor. There they entered their new and furnished apartment.

The interior stunned her. The white modern kitchen came complete with all the appliances. A black leather corner sofa in the living area faced the view from the windows. The tables and cabinets of cherry red, shiny stained wood, combined with glass. It all matched together in perfect harmony. A most extravagant presentation.

She walked towards the sliding doors that opened to a wide balcony. She stepped outside and gazed at the breathtaking view. The beach, the ocean, the palm trees and the surrounding hills and scenery. A scattering of sailing boats moved on the water. A variety of songbirds chanted and called out.

Nathan joined her and put his arms around her.

"Welcome to Sydney, my dear," he said, "are you happy?"

"Yes, I'm happy," she replied, and she kissed him on a cheek. They went back inside to make love on the huge king size bed. Falling sound asleep afterward. Satisfied and tired from the long journey.

Chapter 5

In her sleep, Claire's mind wandered back in time.
Late afternoon, one of her colleagues walked into her office. "Yes, Peter? Is it important? I'm trying to finish an important report!" She looked up at him.
"Sorry, Claire, I didn't mean to disturb you. But the boss asked for you."
"What? Why?"
"I don't know. He wants to talk to you, that's all he said."
"Alright. Tell him I'll be there in a few minutes!"
"You need to come over straight away!" Peter insisted.
"What's so important that it can't wait?" she replied, agitated. She swung her chair backward and rushed towards the door. Peter jumped out of her way.
"You can leave!" she snapped at him. "Thanks!"
Moments later, she reached the office of the Director of the company. She knocked on the door.
"Come in!"
"You wanted to see me, James?"
"Ah! Claire! Yes! What's the status of the Bellamy project you're working on? Are you finished?" He rested his eyes on her.
"Almost," she replied. "I need at least another day!"
"I'm afraid that's not possible! There's a presentation tomorrow morning!" His hands moved over his bold skull.
"Why didn't you tell me this earlier on?" she defied him.
"Because they confirmed it only a moment ago, over the phone!" The muscles in his face showed signs of tension.
"You must finish it today!

Even if it takes you all evening!"

"But James!" she grumbled. "I planned a dinner date!"

"Well, I'm sorry, Claire. You may wish to call it off. This is an important client. Get it done!" He motioned her to the door with his hands. The tone of his voice warned her that any more arguing over the matter became fruitless.

Her initial cheerful mood soon changed into sheer dismay. She wanted to see Mason! She tried to get the job finished in time, but she failed to deliver.

Mason stood preparing their romantic evening meal. Meanwhile listening to love songs by Frank Sinatra.

"You will be impressed with my cooking, my dear Claire," he whispered. "My delightful princess! I'm lucky and yet, will you ever be mine?" He had mixed feelings.

He looked at the clock. It was getting late! Could it be that she had second thoughts? The sound of his phone interrupted.

"Mason, it's me, Claire! I'm so sorry Mason," she began. "I have to cancel our evening together! My boss wants me to finish a special project. I need the rest of the evening to work on it. I tried my best to complete it earlier, but I couldn't."

Her heart sank when he answered somewhat agitated. "Why didn't you call me sooner?" he said, "now dinner is almost ready!" She didn't respond.

"Couldn't you at least come over to eat?" he asked, trying to persuade her. "It will only be an hour and then you can finish your work afterward."

She remained dead silent, and he heard her think on the other side of the phone line before she responded.

Faithless Romance 22

"I better not. I'm afraid it may be longer than an hour and I can't afford to lose any more time! I'll take a rain check!"
He sighed in despair.
"Fine! I understand!" He caved in. "Do what you have to do! I'll pretend you are here with me. The table is set with my best tablecloth, cutlery, and plates. Complete with crystal glasses and candles. I will enjoy the lovely meal by myself. It's a shame to let it go to waste."
"That sounds like a good idea!" she commented, not sure whether he joked or not. "Just out of curiosity, what did you make?"
He laughed out loud. "I won't tell you! Otherwise, I can't surprise you with it the next time. Let me know when you are ready to choose a new date."
"I will!" she said. "I better get back to work. Don't worry, I'll speak to you soon! Kiss, kiss, bye for now!" She ended the conversation to avoid any further discomfort.
"That didn't go down well," she concluded. The call left a bitter after-taste. She contemplated whether to leave the next move to him or not.
Undecided, she concentrated on her present obligations. She spent the rest of the evening at the office, working on the task that she indeed needed to complete.
She jumped up when one of her new co-workers, Nathan Kingsley, attracted her attention.
"Nathan! You scared me! How long did you stand there for? I didn't see or hear you coming!"
"Hello, beautiful!" he said. "I stood watching you for a while. I didn't want to disturb you.
You appeared to be so caught up in your work!"

He entered the room, putting a hand on her right shoulder. "Need any help?" He offered to help her in accomplishing her assignment.

"I guess it's for the Bellamy company?"

"Yes, it is!" she replied. "They came up with a last minute presentation!"

It involved an important account for the firm. Both of them wanted to make their client happy. To offer the best management and marketing plan for growing their customer's business. He sat down on the chair next to her.

Claire took a liking to Nathan, a risk taker, and an adventurer, yet dedicated to the company. His lifestyle and his presence appealed to her.

He displayed a great masculine physique. With his blond hair and sparkling bright blue eyes, he resembled a robust Viking. She loved men that took pride in their appearance and body fitness. Nathan won from Mason in that respect. She adored both men, each for her own specific reasons.

During their late-night session, the brief intimate moments with Nathan affected her. More so when he sat closer to her. Their hands and legs touched often. At long last, their eyes met with such an intensified glare that the next step was inevitable.

Neither of them resisted the longing to kiss one and other. It didn't take long for them to take it a step further. Their love-making was exhilarating, tigerish.

The windows of the room soon filled with steam.

Claire's auburn hair came loose and the curls fell around her face. Her cheeks turned a bright red and her eyes sparkled.

She felt overjoyed once they satisfied their lustful feelings. It stood in sharp contrast to her mood with Mason the other night.

She blossomed under Nathan's charisma, relishing the intense pleasure.

"Right," he said. "Work to be done! I have an amazing idea! Let's discuss it further."

They returned to the table with renewed energy and continued where they left off earlier on. For the moment, she deleted any thoughts about Mason from her mind.

Chapter 6

The explosive evening with Nathan changed Claire's feelings for Mason. The promise to call him for a new date bothered her. She now asked herself whether she wanted to meet him again on such short notice.
Although the romantic attention of both men flattered her, it made matters complicated. She knew Mason meant more than a one-night stand. And, after her fling with Nathan, the thought alone made her wary.
Yet, she saw Mason as a potential husband. She liked his stability and his tenderness. Characteristics that worked like a magnet. Whether his ability to pull her in persuaded her enough to tie the knot? She wavered between the two of them.
But, she connected to both men from a business point of view and she was mindful of that relevance. It could be better to ignore Mason for a while, even though she put herself in a precarious position.
For that reason, she did not respond straight away when he sent her flowers the following day. Although she knew a polite 'thank you' towards a business associate, became unavoidable.
One evening and several days later, she contemplated to call him but didn't. She went to bed early with a book and tried to keep her mind away from him. It wasn't easy. She hoped he understood her silence.
But instead, she received text messages from him. He expressed his concern for her well-being, asking several questions.

"Why didn't you call me? What happened? Have you been in an accident? Or is it something else?"

She sensed his confusion and his displeasure. He wanted answers. He wanted to hear the truth. She had to make a move! The situation worsened by Nathan's efforts to pick up where they left it that one evening.

On a late afternoon, she made up her mind to visit Mason at his shop. Just before closing time, she walked through the door.

She looked ravishing in her coral blue pantsuit and white blouse. Her hair draped loosely around her delicate face. When she entered through the door, he stood perplexed and gazed at her. Her cheeks grew warm, this time turning red with shame.

"Hello Mason," she said in her sweetest voice. "I wanted to thank you in person for the red roses you sent me a while ago. Sorry for the delayed response, but I had to go on an unexpected business trip," she lied.

She walked up to him and kissed him on the mouth, hoping to diminish his anxiety and worries. He stayed unaffected and silent.

"Are you free for dinner?" she then asked, pretending not to notice his sulkiness.

"Well, hello to you too!" he replied irksomely. "What a surprise!" he continued, still angry.

"I'm happy to see you again. And I'm glad you are okay, but you could at least have left me a message to say you were gone for a couple of days!"

"I know," she responded in her most apologetic voice, "I didn't mean to upset you."

Faithless Romance

"But you did," he said resolute, "and, it made me realize how much I missed you," he confessed.

He couldn't help himself. Keeping a distance became impossible, no matter how hard he tried.

His admission startled her. It confused her even more.

"Where do you want to go?" she asked, to try to divert his attention. "There's this small, cozy restaurant, two blocks away from here," she suggested. "That would be perfect!"

"You mean Cortado?" he asked.

"Yes, that's the one!" she replied.

"They do serve great food and a tasteful coffee," he said, "that's nice."

"Then let's go!" She turned a pleased smile on him.

On the way to the restaurant, he took her by the hand. She felt uneasy but kept quiet.

She soon embraced the renewed sensation of his touch. And for the moment, her fling with Nathan got pushed away. She wasn't sure how to further handle him, but that was of a later concern.

She could no longer deny that both males attracted her, be it in a different way. Nathan full of life and sexuality, and not the type to get involved in a long relationship. Mason calm, serious and more sensitive.

But, she'd have to make a choice, or not? A question difficult to answer right now.

When they had ordered their meal she said, "I made a new interior design drawing for your shop.

You can have an even better display of your jewelry that way. And," she added, "I devised a new ad campaign for you. I hope you appreciate it."

She handed him a ready-made presentation.

Mason marveled at the way she took the initiative.

The unexpected announcement stunned him. It pleased him that she worked on his business venture.

"Is this what you occupied yourself with during your trip?" he asked, delighted.

"You developed a marketing plan for my business, as you promised! That's fantastic!" he responded overjoyed.

He glanced at it and most of her recommendations and ideas surprised and pleased him.

"Do you mind if I take it with me and study it in more detail later tonight, at home?" he requested and glared at her.

"Of course not," she replied. "It's not something you can decide on straight away. I understand." She gave him the material.

"Let me know what you think and don't hesitate to comment or change anything," she continued.

"Don't worry, I won't!" he said with determination.

She remained silent, at a loss for words. She smiled at him. Her lips parted, and she moisturized them with the tip of her tongue.

The movement triggered his primal lust. He began to breathe heavy and his sweat glands worked overtime.

"Are you alright?" she asked him in her most sensuous voice. "You look flushed."

Her intense hazelnut brown eyes were now fixed on his face. She got worried and concerned for his well-being.

"Yes, I'm fine," he replied flustered. "It's hard to believe we only met a few days ago.

Faithless Romance

It seems as if I've known you forever!" he conjured up as an excuse.

"Perhaps we do," she giggled, "from another lifetime," she said, now more serious.

"The idea of reincarnation appeals to me. What about you?" Once more, she let her gaze on his face.

"I never gave that any thought, to be honest," he admitted. "Interesting that you mention that. Who knows! Life is full of mysteries! Whatever is the reason, I'm grateful that you walked into my life. And I'm hopeful you will stay in it forever!"

She didn't respond. Instead, she looked at her watch.

"Oh no!" she exclaimed. "It's late! I have to go! I'm sorry Mason. It's an early start tomorrow and I need my beauty sleep!" She chuckled.

Astounded by her own sudden mood change, she got up. As a gallant gentleman, he moved her chair backward so she could leave the table. He helped her into her coat.

She saw he hesitated to ask her the question that burned on his lips.

"When will we get together again?" He looked anxious, waiting for her forthcoming reply.

"I can't say," she replied, and she touched his hand.

"Sorry Mason, I just can't. Don't take it the wrong way, but I have many commitments lined up this week. I promise I will call you as soon as I'm available."

She gave him a soft kiss on the mouth.

He stood frozen to the ground, overcome with her unexpected cool attitude. Yet, he managed to compose himself.

Faithless Romance 30

He tried hard not to show his utter disappointment.
"Don't leave me in the dark too long!" he said, joking around, "otherwise I may get lost!"
She frowned her thin eyebrows.
"Don't worry," she replied, "I'll lead you the way!"
With these mystifying words, she left him to his own devices. She was well aware of the fact that she just gave him the runaround. He wondered whether she played games with him, but what was she supposed to do? It troubled her, and she was gutted.
Why did she have the feeling that she had to take matters into her own hands? Why didn't he argue with her or try to convince her to make time available for him?
Why was he so accommodating? She didn't understand him! She had to think long and hard over the next few days. That much was certain.
Tormented, she left the restaurant.

Faithless Romance

Chapter 7

When Claire got home, she went for a drive. Appalled by her standoffish behavior towards Mason. She never intended to hurt him, but the way he spoke to her triggered her off. His facial expression told her more than enough to justify her response.

She invoked an unexpected turnaround for both of them. His adoration for her went beyond the pure and the physical. That development scared her the most. Her emotions ran high. It puzzled her and caused her to answer his kindness with disrespect.

She wanted someone like Nathan, strong and handsome. An outgoing, adventurous and career-focused guy. Assertive and straightforward.

Mason provided the absolute opposite. Plain looks, somewhat shy, and dull. But he gave stability, security, and everlasting love instead.

And that worries me, she reasoned. I can't settle down yet. What about my career? The places I want to visit and discover? Is Mason a person to allow me to carry on the way I want to? She sighed.

Loud sirens of a police car interrupted her deliberations. The car came up right behind her, with high speed and signaled her to stop at the side of the road.

"Now what!" she murmured, annoyed. "Just my luck!"

She moved the car to the verge and waited.

A police officer walked up to her and shone his flashlight onto her face, which blinded her. She moved her hands above her eyes to block out the bright light.

"Good evening, Ma'am," he said. "Can I see your drivers license, please?"

"Of course!" She smiled and doted on him. "Is there something wrong, officer?" she asked in her most innocent voice.

"I'm afraid there is, Ma'am," he replied. "You ignored a red traffic light earlier on. Any ongoing traffic and you wouldn't be talking right now. It must have been your lucky day. Because this is a busy intersection."

Claire responded overwhelmed. "Are you sure officer?" she pouted. "I can't recall any red light at all! I'm always so careful when I drive!" She flirted with him to avoid getting fined.

"I hope you can forgive me for this unintended oversight?" she went on, meanwhile leaning out of the car window.

This guy looks stunning in his uniform, she deduced. Look at those broad shoulders and that jaw line!

He glanced at her drivers' license and then back at her. "Please step out of the car!" he commanded.

"But officer!" she pleaded.

"Now Ma'am, if you please!" he continued, not taking no for an answer.

"Oh! I love it when they use their authority! It makes him even more attractive!" He turned her on.

In slow motion, she moved her gorgeous legs out of the car door, one by one. She pretended to fall over and fell right against his chest.

He grabbed her arm and a pair of bright blue eyes stared into hers. She heard her own heartbeat, loud and fast.

Faithless Romance

"Please don't hurt me," she begged him. But her body language showed what she expected from him.

He threw her against her car, spread her legs and forced her arms against the metal. He pressed his masculine body against hers. His hand touched her private parts. She didn't mind it at all!

"Oh officer!" she cooed, "this is a great traffic stop!"

Her whole body shivered when he made his final move. She needed this, after her unsatisfying evening with Mason. This was pure lust, pure indulgence! It was sublime!

"Right!" the officer said when they finished. He looked at her, resolute yet tender. "I will only give you a warning this time. It may be a whole different story when I catch you again," he grinned.

"My name and phone number are on the back." He handed her a piece of paper. "In case you need the help of the police sometime soon."

"Well thank you, officer," she crowed, "I'm much obliged!"

"Have a nice continuation of the evening, Ma'am," he said. "Goodbye!"

"Goodbye!" she whispered, meanwhile getting back into her car. She looked in her rear-view mirror. Her skin glowed, her eyes flickered.

"My goodness, what a turn of events!" she mumbled, "or rather what an electrifying one-night stand!"

It gave her a sense of much-needed sexual relief.

"But, what came over me? Why did I let it happen? Things are complicated enough!" She groaned.

Faithless Romance

What's the matter with me? She asked herself.

She had to get a hold of herself after this short and wild affair at the roadside. In hindsight, her own conduct disgusted her. To get carried away, and to behave as a prostitute! How sickening!

Not to mention her mixed feelings for Nathan and Mason. She found herself torn between the two of them. At age twenty-four, she needed permanence in her life. Mason offered her that chance, but should she take it?

Do I want to continue my life with Nathan or with Mason? she wondered. Or do I want to be as free as a butterfly? And, whatever happens, happens?

She crumpled the note with the phone number and threw it away. Her inner questions remained unanswered and kept her occupied for days.

It turned out to be a stressful and agonizing week. She then made the crucial decision to change her life forever! To find out whether he was the one! So, she called him.

"Mason, it's Claire! I want to apologize for my conduct in the restaurant and for leaving the way I did."

She didn't wait for his response and continued.

"I needed time to reflect, on my career, my life, and our first meeting. I must admit, I'm confused. I'm not sure if we should continue our ongoing relationship."

The fact that she called it a relationship made her committed to him.

No doubt he'll be happy about my admission that I do care for him! she reckoned.

It meant a significant step forward. It required careful deliberation before taking it a step further.

Faithless Romance

She gave him the opportunity to respond.

He didn't disappoint her.

"I'm grateful that you are honest with me," he replied most sincere. "I understand you! I'm as confused as you are! After all, we collided in the street, only a short while ago. From then on, we took a rapid journey into the unknown, with no proper preparation!"

"That's right!" she responded in good spirits. "I'm so glad you see it that way!" A broad smile formed around her mouth and she couldn't stop smiling.

"How do you suggest we continue our journey?" he asked.

She sensed that he wanted her to make the next move. He understood that she needed control and independence. That he couldn't tie her down. This time she was grateful for his lack of initiative.

She recognized his acknowledgment, knowing the decision to move forward lay in her hands. He longed to be with her, but he waited for her reaction.

"Well," she answered his question. "Why don't you come over to my apartment next Friday and stay the weekend? To explore and to set out the best route for us to take from then on."

He didn't respond at first. Was it too much too soon? She couldn't imagine he rejected her offer. She asked him to sleep with her! So, why the hesitation?

Even though she liked being in charge, she now felt less reassured.

"Are you still there, Mason?" she asked, irritated. "Mason?"

At long last, he snapped out of his short delusional state and he responded exhilarated.

"Yes Claire, I'm here and I'm delighted! I'll come over and stay with you!"

"Thank you!" she said lighthearted, yet with a strong voice. "Thank you for understanding!"

"Not a problem!" he said. "I look forward to seeing you again."

"Good, I'm glad I called," she concluded. "See you in a few days time! Bye for now." She ended the call and sat in silence for a while.

This is my last chance to make it work, she pondered.

I know he'll do everything to make me happy. But, is that enough for me? She wished she knew the answer.

Oblivious to her confusion, Mason regained his confidence, adamant to make this weekend a success. He wanted to show her how much she meant to him, without smothering her or without chasing her away from him.

Chapter 8

When the momentous weekend arrived, Claire felt joyful but uptight. Her face reflected signs of worry and tension in the mirror. She recognized the fear. A clear apprehension to take the relationship with Mason to the next level.

Her dilemma at this point led her into further doubts. She even considered canceling the whole stopover.

"I need to listen to my heart, not my mind!" she spoke to her glass counterpart. "I'm irrational! Although he brings out feelings within me, I'm not head over heels in love with him! But, he worships me, and he cares for me! Besides, his jewelry store means a business challenge and financial gain!"

Her occasional flings with other men gave her nothing in return but sexual satisfaction. She wanted and needed more at this point.

If I want stability in my life, I have to commit myself to one man! I have to show him my inmost affection and understanding, whatever happens!

A dangerous path to follow. It could be difficult for her to give him her full devotion. She'd find it hard to resist her everlasting adoration for other men, no matter what!

After an hour of deliberation, she decided she had to take the chance. She promised herself to stay on guard, to avoid any thoughtless remarks. Never to allow Mason to doubt his own judgment in agreeing to stay with her during the forthcoming days.

Late that afternoon, he arrived at her apartment.

Still unconvinced and wavering, her heart beat accelerated when she opened the door. Her concerns proved unfounded.

"Hello again! Here I am!" He greeted her with an affectionate smile. The same smile that he gave her when they first met. The one that won her over when she searched for her bracelet.

The same self-assured appearance, looking handsome in light gray pants and a multicolored shirt!

"Hello to you too!" she grinned. "I'm glad you could make it!" She sounded provocative.

Her seductive tone made him kiss her with wild passion once he stood inside the hallway. Her earlier worries faded away. She wondered why she lacked confidence in him. He swept her off her feet.

She forgot her safeguard and surrendered to her ecstasy. This time, Mason unleashed the tiger within her! She never thought that possible!

An amazing few days followed. They explored each others' limits and discovered new common ground.

"Tell me, how was your childhood?" she asked him at one point. "Were you a happy child? Are your parents still alive?"

"There's not much to tell in a way," he replied. "As an only child, both my parents got killed in a car accident. It caused a tremendous change in my young adult life, at the age of nineteen." She could see the hurt in his eyes.

"I'm so sorry to hear that," she said.

"Before the incident, I enjoyed the good times," he continued.

Faithless Romance

"Happy-go-lucky, I used to help out in the jewelry store of my father, together with my mother.
A real family business, one that I inherited when they passed away. I learned the tricks of the trade from my father. My mother taught me the importance of customer relations! To hold a smile on your face, no matter what. And to always remain polite to our customers."
Claire listened with interest and compassion.
He pulled her closer, and she nestled herself in his arms. He went on.
"Through the years, after my parents' death, I attended several business courses. I presented the business at jewelry events. Essential to keep up to date with the ever changing market!"
She nodded in agreement.
"A hectic but lonely period. That's why I want more permanence now! I'm twenty-eight. It's time to have a soul mate! Someone to share my ups and downs! Maybe even start a family of my own!"
Claire wasn't sure whether to embrace this suggestion. Such a big step meant huge responsibilities. Yet the idea to settle down became more and more appealing.
It's time to make up my mind, she told herself. Stop procrastinating!
On their last day together, a hint of nervousness hung around Mason. Later that afternoon, she found out why.
She got an enormous surprise when he went down on his knees and said; "Claire, I love you. Every minute, every second of the day, you are on my mind. I can't imagine my life without you anymore!

Faithless Romance *40*

This weekend has only confirmed my loving feelings for you. Will you please marry me?"

He took her hands and looked at her, showing his devotion.

The bombshell caught her off-balance.

"Mason! Isn't it too early for you to ask?" she replied, still shaken. The euphoria of the moment slipped away.

She saw him swallow a few times, in suspense of her further response. He looked apprehensive, and she understood why. Their future lay in her hands.

She bowed her head to regain her composure. When she recovered, she looked straight into his eyes. She caressed his hands when she answered, calm and serene. "But, of course, I accept!"

"For real?" he jumped up, ecstatic. He couldn't believe his luck.

"That's fantastic! You had me worried there for a moment, my love! I thought you were going to decline my offer!" His lips formed a wide and happy smile when he took a small red case out of his pocket. Once he opened it, a small gold ring with tiny diamonds appeared.

He took her left hand and put the ring on her finger. "With this ring, I thee wed," he whispered.

"Oh, Mason!" she gloated, "it's gorgeous!" She admired the jewel on her hand. It sparkled in the afternoon sun and it astonished her. She couldn't believe he came prepared.

"It matches your mother's bracelet," he explained. He demonstrated a keen eye for detail.

"Thank you, that's so thoughtful of you!" She kissed him, excited and desirous.

He responded with great eagerness.

Fate brought them together, and they ended up as a couple. Still reluctant, she hoped she made the right decision. At least, she won herself over, soon to become Mrs. Claire Brannigan! Despite her doubts and reservations, it felt justifiable, for now.

They decided to get married in the next twelve months.

She never imagined in her wildest dreams to marry someone like Mason.

I hope I have the guts to see it through, she reflected, and to make it last.

Chapter 9

During the weeks following his proposal, Claire became increasingly worried and insecure. Did she make the right decision? She tossed around with the idea to cancel their marriage plans. Nathan couldn't believe it either when she told him of her intentions.
"You are out of your mind!" he responded in anger. "What got into you? You and I are a team! This is so not you, Claire! You will regret this, I'm telling you!" His resistive reaction made it the more difficult.
"Why aren't you happy for me?" she asked him. "I want a stable and secure life!" She tried to explain it to him, but it was of no use.
"Don't blame me afterward," he said, "I warned you. It won't last!" She hurt his ego, and he persevered in trying to win her back.
In the meantime, Mason enjoyed their engagement period as much as possible. In the back of his mind, he worried over Claire's promise and devotion.
He soon became aware of the depth and nature of her character. Independence remained of importance to her. Her business drive and ambitions became clear.
His shop thrived under her management and they started a franchise chain. They opened more jewelry stores throughout the city. Although she agreed to move in with him, she insisted on keeping her own job. She wanted to be independent.
Six months into the course of their engagement, trouble began.

"It's time we plan our wedding," he said one evening. "We're getting closer to the end of the twelve months. And, I'd love to have children soon after! How about you?"

"Well, I'd say that can wait," she figured. "I'm still in my early twenties. There's plenty of time. Even for you!"

She treasured her career. That side of their future together did not appeal to her. At least, not at the moment.

They always ended up arguing over the matter. It strained their relationship.

She realized that they lost interest in each other, more and more. Their time spent together slacked up. Often, she dreaded going home. So she worked late evenings.

During those late hours, Nathan grabbed the chance to join her. With the excuse, he wanted to help her to finish a project. He once promised himself he would win her back, and he embraced the opportunity.

He knew Claire couldn't withstand his amorous advances if he persisted. And before long, they started an affair.

"Why do you always work late?" Mason confronted her with her awkward behavior.

"It's about time you stand up to your boss! Our own business should have your priority! I wonder if you're hiding something from me!"

Claire waved it aside.

"Your imagination runs wild with you!" she told him. "Our firm gained many new clients, which means extra work at the office," she explained.

"It requires my full attention! I need to work overtime to complete the several assignments.

Faithless Romance

Besides, we can put that extra money to good use!"

"Are you sure you are telling me the truth, Claire?" he spoke with doubt in his voice. Unconvinced by her story, Mason became most suspicious.

"I smelled a distinctive aftershave on your clothes! Other than my own!" He presumed she lied to him.

He tried to figure out whether she worked on the job those late nights or whether she cheated on him.

She became angry.

"Are you calling me a liar?" she snapped at him. "Did you ever consider the scent comes from one of my customers? They sometimes sit up close!" Her explanation didn't persuade him.

Soon after their argument, he called her at work, for no reason. She realized that he tried to pick up sounds from her surroundings during those conversations. Voices or noises that proved to him she had company.

She tried her utmost to convince him that his lack of faith was irrational.

His next step was a bold one.

Much later she found out he undertook this action to find out if his suspicions were unfounded or not.

One evening, he decided to pay her a surprise visit at the office, bringing her a special takeaway meal. The security guard downstairs recognized him so it was easy to get through the door.

He got into the elevator and went up to her bureau, on the fourth floor of the building. Cautious, he stepped into the corridor on her level. He remained on guard and advanced towards the glass front of her room.

When he saw her sitting at her desk, it relieved him. She told the truth, she worked overtime!

He wanted to open the door to surprise her, but a shadow appeared at her right-hand side. The shadow of a familiar person. He recognized him as Nathan Kingsley, his adversary.

Earlier in their relationship, Claire introduced him to Nathan at a corporate event. She confessed at the time that she once had a sexual affair with the blond pretender.

Mason watched his rival bend over to his soon to be wife. He caressed her hair, took the pen out of her hand and turned her chair, making her face him. He then took her face in his hands and kissed her so intense that Mason wobbled on his feet.

Right there and then, his heart broke into thousands of tiny pieces. Devastated by the tragic experience, he put the meal near the door. He left the building, torn up and distressed.

Back at home, he crash-landed in his favorite chair and poured himself a full glass of bourbon. He sat there for hours, staring into nothing, drinking to gain courage while he waited for her to come home.

Later that evening, unaware of his grim mood, Claire turned the key in the front door lock. When she stepped inside he looked fierce, without greeting her, as usual. Instead, he sighed the deepest sigh. She smiled at him but he remained sullen.

"Did you find your surprise meal at the office?" he asked her casual. His question took her by surprise.

"What do you know about my meal?" she wondered.

"That's obvious, isn't it?" he commented, complacent. "I put it there!"

"Oh?" she said, unsure how to respond. "But I didn't see you!"

"No, of course not!" he replied with sarcasm. "You were too busy kissing Nathan, weren't you?"

Her mouth fell open. His revelation knocked her down.

"So you found out!"

She sighed and plopped into the chair next to him. "I'm sorry Mason. One day, I would have told you!" She tried to soften the blow.

"Well, thank God for that!" he said, his voice now getting louder. "Am I supposed to feel better now!?"

She bent her head, afraid to look him in the eyes. Nervous, she fumbled with her fingers.

"I guess not," she whispered.

"No!" he shouted and got out of his chair. He paced up and down the room.

"How could you Claire! After everything that we've shared! How could you! I remember you once said this Nathan guy was a no-good-for-nothing so and so. A charlatan, a womanizer and more. Now you have an affair with him! All those evenings, working late?" He paused, then continued.

"And you know what the worst part is, Claire?" He looked at her with a stern face. "You lied! You pretended nothing was wrong, that we were good! Have I got news for you, my dear! I never believed you, although I wanted to! But, deep in my heart, I knew it! I knew the day would come that you'd betray me. You've always been footloose.

You proved that I was right. You seemed happy and content with me. But you chose to stab me in the back. How stupid of me! My mistake!"

His head pounded, his heart tore during his further outburst.

"I've given you everything that I can! There's nothing more. What do you want Claire? Where did we go astray?"

She now got up and walked towards him with tears in her eyes.

"You're not at fault, Mason. You are not the one to blame. It's me! I wished to settle down, but I'm restless! Your love and security should be enough for me, but it isn't! I need adventure, passion, danger! That's what I find with Nathan."

She tried to take his hand, but he pulled away. There was no way he let her touch him at this point.

"Nathan suggested we elope to Australia," she said. "I guess I better accept his proposal."

"Yes, you should!" he replied, angry and sick at heart at the same time.

"Marriage is not right for us. I hope you find the happiness you search for Claire!"

He turned around and walked away to their spare bedroom. No longer able to face her, or to listen to her. The agony tore him apart.

She heard him sob in silence behind the closed door, forever a broken man.

Chapter 10

A month later in Sydney. Claire woke up. A soft breeze with hot air blew in from the ocean. An invitation to share breakfast on the terrace. A delightful start of the day.

"I'll get us four fresh croissants from the nearby bakery!" Nathan announced. "And a carton of orange juice. I will pick up two coffee to go from the local dairy!" His prior knowledge of the area became evident.

"What a splendid way to begin our new life together!" she responded. She listened to the early morning sounds. Refusing to think about Mason.

When Nathan returned from his errands, they enjoyed their delicious early meal at the seaside.

The rest of the day they strolled around to explore their surroundings. After a delicious lunch at Julio's Seafood Beach Restaurant, they went grocery shopping.

The following days, they toured around Sydney. They visited the botanical gardens and the Opera House. Took a trip on the ferry around the harbor and went on a shopping spree in the town center. They had a fabulous time. Claire lived the dream. She relished it.

"It's a shame it comes to an end!" she commented when they read the Sunday paper together. 'Time to get back to work tomorrow!"

Nathan looked up and agreed. "It is, isn't it? Oh well, it's been fun! That's for sure! Besides, we can continue this lifestyle during the weekends and the holidays!"

Baxter Corporate Management held their Sydney office in Martin Place, in the town center.

Not having a car turned out to be inconvenient.
But they had to accept it for a few weeks.
Nathan convinced her to secure and ask for a sum of Mason's business proceeds. She helped grow his business. And she earned the right to get the money. The additional funds would make her new life here more comfortable.
She regretted her unfaithfulness to Mason, but Nathan's suggestion made sense. She'd put it away for a rainy day. Financial security for unforeseen circumstances.
She went to see a lawyer and started the legal process. But she asked the counselor to be fair. She didn't want Mason to suffer more than need be.
After a while, life became a routine, even in such a wonderful place on earth. Though Nathan made sure not to miss out on fun and excitement. If he had any spare time, he either went surfing or sailing with his mates. He played golf, and tennis or anything else he fancied.
Although Claire joined him now and then, she disliked his frequent outings. It irritated her. She lost the willingness to go along with his loose conduct. They argued often because she stood up to his macho behavior and irresponsible attitude.
He became way too obsessed with his looks and his body. More than once, she caught him flirting with other women. He beat her at her own game.
"Do you have to behave towards women like that?" she confronted him one day.
"Like what?" he asked, insensible to her feelings.
"Flirting and enticing," she clarified, "you know what I mean!"

Faithless Romance

"No, I'm sorry, I don't," he flat-out denied any knowledge of the matter. "Don't be ridiculous. What is it with you? You don't want to do this, you don't want to do that and now you're accusing me of flirting? Get over it woman! Besides, may I remind you, you used to do the same?"

Angry, he marched away, grabbed his car keys and took off, who knows where.

He left Claire rattled. She longed back to her calm and more relaxed life in England with Mason. At a loss, she asked herself where to go from here.

So it came as a shock to her when Mason forced her to make a short-term decision. What share did she want from his business? His lawyer informed her he intended to marry someone else!

What did I expect? she thought. That he sits around and waits for me, forever? Only now did she realize that she indeed expected that of him. It never crossed her mind he would consider marriage again. Not after their disastrous engagement!

For an awkward reason, she felt jealous and spiteful. She even contemplated not to sign the papers and ask for more money. But at last, she came to her senses. It wouldn't be fair towards him. He deserved a new chance for happiness in his life after what she'd put him through.

She signed the documents, and that was that.

Two nights later, Nathan came home from another outing with his mates. An upset Claire shouted at him.

"Well, well!" she yelled, "it's time you came home, Nathan! You seem to forget that you are in a relationship with me!

I do not wish to spend every evening or every weekend on my own. That's not why I joined you to move to Australia!"

He looked stunned and threw his gear in the corner of the room, fired up and angry. His reply sarcastic.

"How lovely to see you too!" he responded.

"You're not starting an argument again, are you? As far as I remember, I have been home the last two evenings! I always go out with the guys on Friday's! Why make such a fuzz about it?" He went over to the fridge and grabbed himself a beer.

"Didn't you drink enough?" she asked provoked. "You came home from the pub! You smell like it!"

"Yes, and?" he questioned her. "Do you think I can't handle it or something? Gosh, you sound like a sour housewife!"

He plopped down on the couch and drank the bottle of alcohol empty in one go.

"Come, sit next to me," he invited her over. "Don't be such a spoil sport. Make it up!"

His eyes glowed, and she recognized his boozed, playful and irritating mood.

Something clicked in her head. His attitude and his actions disgusted her. He treated her like a call girl! In no way could he persuade her!

"Have I got news for you!" she said, offended. "Forget it! Forget us, and this!" she pointed to the furniture. "This is not my life, it's yours! I've had it!

Go ahead, be the happy-go-lucky bachelor! Have it your way! But I'm out of here by tomorrow!"

Faithless Romance 52

She turned around and went to the spare bedroom. Slammed and locked the door behind her.

Nathan followed her. For a while, he pleaded in front of the door. He wanted her to come out and make amends.

But she refused to give in.

She got fed up with the arguments. And fed up with his drunken moods and his extreme, destructive male egocentrism.

I don't know where to go from here, she thought, but I'll figure it out tomorrow morning.

The following day, she felt undetermined. She heard Nathan. He was already up and about. It being a Saturday, he prepared to go out for his usual surfing session.

He shouted at her through the door.

"Are you still in there? Answer me, Claire! Get over it! Don't be childish! Have some fun yourself! You need it!"

She heard him make breakfast in the kitchen and next he took a shower. Then the front door opened and closed again. He left without an apology. Without trying to persuade her once more, to come out of the room.

She now faced a real dilemma.

"What is the matter with me?" she wondered, puzzled. "Plenty of men out there and I adore men! And what did I expect from Nathan? I preferred an outgoing guy! Then why is it a problem?" She couldn't answer that question.

All she knew was that it threw her off balance right now and she wanted a change.

It even meant getting another job.

She couldn't bare the thought of working alongside Nathan. Not after all that happened between them.

Faithless Romance

For a while, she remained in the room. She sat on the bed, contemplating what to do next.

After a few hours of deliberation, she began packing her suitcases. Nathan would stay out all day, so she had plenty of time to gather her belongings.

"How lucky I saved the money I got out of the business venture with Mason!" she uttered. "I need it right now!"

She planned to first stay in a holiday rental for a couple of weeks and quit her job. That over and done with, the search for a long-term rental apartment began.

She had to find another company to work for.

Both tasks wouldn't be easy, but she had to start somewhere. Staying around with Nathan horrified her. Better to leave today than to procrastinate.

Once she packed her belongings, she loaded everything in her blue Toyota Auris. She drove to the holiday apartment in Double Bay, that she found on the internet.

She left a small note for Nathan.

"When you read this, I'm gone. Our relationship isn't working out. I don't see a future for us together. Take care."

She took one last look at the luxury she left behind and she placed the short letter on the kitchen bar.

Chapter 11

Despite this sad turn of events, Claire welcomed her decision. She became excited about the near future.
"The change may bring opportunities my way," she murmured. "There's always something positive to learn from a negative situation."
Pleased with her own willpower, she enjoyed the short journey to Double Bay. The stylish, harbor-side eastern suburb of Sydney lay closer to the central business district. Home to lush parks, tree-lined boulevards, grand residences and luxurious penthouses.
With bustling pavement cafes and exclusive boutiques. She looked forward to visiting them all.
When she arrived at the Bellevue Hill Garden Apartment, she got a pleasant surprise. She loved the spacious rooms with the stunning timber floors.
The two well-sized bedrooms turned out to be bright and cozy. The lounge provided comfort and the kitchen-diner invited her to cook. From the window, she viewed the park across the road, but she also had a private garden.
She wouldn't mind staying here for a while, but it cost a hundred and seventy dollars per night. Too expensive for the long term.
Straight away, she unpacked her clothes and other items. And arranged everything in the cupboards available.
She poured herself a glass of white wine, switched on the television and turned her mobile phone off.
Unintended, she mused over the past. The days she spent evenings like this with Mason.

Rather ironic that she found herself in this same position again.

She didn't care about Nathan at all. He got what he deserved. It made her realize that he never meant that much to her as Mason did.

A superficial relationship based on empty promises and sheer sexual attraction. His looks and lifestyle lured her into his arms. Because of him, she lost a real, meaningful and loving relationship.

At least, she now knew the difference. Whether she learned enough and whether she avoided making the same mistake again? A whole different matter altogether.

I still need excitement, she concluded, but it has to be at the right dosage. Maybe it's different when the real Mr. Right comes along, she convinced herself.

After a good night's sleep, she got the morning paper to start her search for a new home and a new career.

The minute she turned on her mobile phone, several text messages from Nathan popped up. He pleaded with her to come back and talk it over. She shrugged her shoulders. Not a chance! In no way, she wanted to speak to him. She returned his messages with one line: "Forget it! Have a nice life!"

She spent all Sunday browsing through the advertisements for a nice apartment. She highlighted a few of them to visit the coming week.

On Monday morning, she went to the office as early as possible, to avoid running into Nathan. She knew he never came in earlier than 9 am. Their general manager did, so she could speak to him about her resigning.

"John, can I have a word?" she asked him when she arrived.

"Yes," he replied, "what can I do for you?"

"I'm afraid I have bad news," she said. "I will have to quit my job with the firm."

"What?" he responded, flabbergasted. "No! You can't be serious, Claire!" His eyes fired up with disbelief.

"But I am!" she continued. "Dead serious! I'm sorry John."

"Please sit down," he invited her. "At least tell me the reason. You seemed to be happy with us and you are delivering such fantastic work. What went wrong?"

For a moment, she hesitated. But then she told him about her breakup with Nathan and what she had been through over the past few months.

When she finished her personal sage, John responded. "Now I understand why Nathan hasn't been functioning well!" he said. "That explains a lot. On more than one occasion, I suspected he sat drunk behind his desk in the afternoon. That must have been so, hearing your stories about him."

He turned silent, and it became clear to Claire that he considered his options.

"I can't afford to lose you, Claire," he announced. "You are way too valuable to the firm! But Nathan is of no particular benefit to us at the moment, the way he is behaving, being irresponsible. So I will fire Nathan and I hope you will stay on, Claire!" He waited for her reaction.

"Are you sure about this?" She wanted confirmation. "Nathan always has brilliant ideas!"

"He *had* great ideas!" John emphasized, "of late, not that many I must confess. Claire, you are a much greater asset to the firm at this point! You are welcome to take a week's holiday from today. In the meantime, I make sure Nathan packs his belongings and leaves. He won't be there when you return, I promise!" He smiled when he said, "and I even give you a pay rise!"

An offer she couldn't refuse.

"Fine!" she answered. "Thank you for your trust and support, I appreciate it!"

"You are most welcome," her boss replied. "You better get out of here, before he walks in. Come back in ten days time!"

She got up from her chair and walked towards the door.

"Thanks again John," she said before she left, "until next week!"

She hurried to leave the building. In the elevator, she recollected the conversation with her boss. The fact that she made Nathan redundant, bothered her. It had not been her intention. Yet, he got it coming and it pleased her she didn't have to go job hunting anymore.

That gave her peace of mind after the recent troubles.

She enjoyed having the week off and apart from looking at apartments, she made use of the shops in the area. Visited the parks and even dared to go to a bar or two at night.

During those outings, she met a few interesting men. They complimented her and their comments elated her.

She exchanged phone numbers and promised to catch up with each of them at a later date.

Faithless Romance

As days passed, she bounced back to her old self.
But despite all that, Mason remained in the back of her mind, no matter how hard she tried to forget him.
"We may meet again one day," she envisioned hopeful, "when we're old and gray!" A faint smile appeared around her mouth. But, she struggled to let it go. She daydreamed about him. More than she wanted to.
I sure made a mess of my life, she concluded dismayed.
I walked into the arms of a wonderful, caring man. I built up a retail jewelry chain, and I ruined it because I wanted to have more excitement!? And what did it bring me? It sucks! She couldn't accept that her efforts to change her life were fruitless.
I could write him! she considered. Tell him that I'm sorry that I hurt him! Maybe there's a slight chance we become friends again! She switched on her tablet to send him an email. She wrote:
"*Dear Mason,*
It has been two years since my departure. You are often on my mind. I hope you and Emily are happy together.
What I did and what I've put you through, is unacceptable. And I long for you to forgive me. Nathan and I broke up. As it turned out he changed for the worse. He hurt me. So I left. I live on my own in a lovely apartment in Double Bay, Sydney. It is my greatest wish you and I can be on speaking terms with each other. To leave the past behind us and move forward. I hope to hear from you.
Yours forever, Claire."

She read it over once more. She hesitated before she pushed the send button, wishing he would reply.

But the days and weeks passed without an answer.

He shunned her. But she remained headstrong to get in touch with him.

One Sunday morning, she wrote his best friend and neighbor Leonardo Stevens, who she met on several occasions during their relationship. She tried to explain it to him. And asked him whether he could speak to Mason on her behalf. This time, she got a reply, the next day.

He told her how sorry he was that things didn't work out with Mason. He found happiness again with Emily. But, he added, Emily turned out to be a most sensitive person and prone to depression and anxieties. She already tried to commit suicide once. They were desperate to have children but she couldn't conceive. And this brought another considerable blow to her already fragile state of mind.

Claire's heart ached for them. She had the greatest sympathy for her ex.

Poor Mason, she grieved. First I broke his heart. And now his new wife brings him nothing but heartbreak! How awful! Oh, Mason, you don't deserve this! No, you don't deserve this at all! If only you'd let me come back into your life! Then I can make it up to you! I can make life more bearable, she reasoned.

Even if I have to play the second violin! she decided. I'll do anything to see you through this, if only you will let me! She wrote another email to Leonardo. To further explain it to him.

Faithless Romance

Chapter 12

Claire could expect another direction in her life. But she continued going through rental announcements. With the help of real estate agents, she looked at potential new living quarters for herself.
Although she considered buying at first, it could be too early for that kind of a commitment. A long term rental arrangement suited her just fine at this moment.
It still could take months before she received any response from Mason. And the present apartment became too expensive. Besides, it was for holidays, not for permanent residency. Finally, her search paid off and she found a perfect match.
The luxury apartment came furnished. The classic yet modern building lay well within a short distance of the bay, beaches, and shops. A perfect location, in the same area as her temporary holiday home.
A stylish and roomy apartment, full of charm and character. With two bedrooms, a modern bathroom, spacious kitchen, parking and small garden. A wonderful and delightful flat.
She wondered whether Nathan still resided in their previous condo, now that he lost his job.
"Why should I care?" she asked herself, "he got what he deserved. I need to focus on my own future!"
She enjoyed the nightlife of Double Bay. During her outings, she met Rick, at the Bluebeat Bar and Grill. Tall, dark and rugged looks, unshaven.

He impressed her with his laid-back attitude and he turned out to be a great dancer.

They met on a regular basis and she got a kick out of his undemanding demeanor. She allowed him to kiss her, but she avoided the more intimate pleasures. Something that she found hard to do. Yet she owed it to herself, to take time out in that respect.

With the pay raise her boss gave her, also came a promotion. She got appointed as the Head of Marketing and Advertising and she loved it. She had regular meetings with top clients of the firm. Dinner parties, gala evenings and charity events to attend.

She was grateful for the full agenda as it didn't allow her to stop and think about Mason or Nathan too often.

Until she ran into Nathan during one of the charity functions! An inconvenient coincidence and quite a shock. Though she had to admit that he looked as handsome as ever. The black smoking he wore suited him. His presence amazed her and her fantasy ran wild.

She pictured him as James Bond and herself as the villain mistress. Ready to lure him into her arms. To then make him suffer and cause him serious harm. As a kind of payback for what he did to her.

She snapped out of her daydream when he approached her. He caught her off guard and it startled her.

"Well, hello, my vicious pussycat!" he confronted her. He sounded and swaggered intoxicated. He swayed with the glass of champagne in front of her and in a reflex she backed away.

"Not so fast!" he sneered and grabbed her by the arm.

"It seems to me we have some issues to resolve between us, Madam!" he slurred.

"Nathan, please! This is not the time nor the place to make a scene!" she begged him.

"Of course not!" he responded agitated, meanwhile dragging her to a quiet corner of the room.

"Was it necessary to have me fired from the job Claire? Was it?" He hissed like a snake, ready to attack its prey. He tightened his grip on her arm.

"Nathan! You are hurting me!" She tried to pull away from him.

"I don't care!" he responded with a double tongue. "It's time for revenge, Claire! Do you have any idea what you've done to me?" he questioned her. "Well? Do you?"

"What I have done to you!?" she replied, filled with anger. "As I recall, you were the one that treated me like a piece of furniture or toy or whatever you want to call it! When you no longer needed me, you threw me into a corner and left me to rot!" With a jerk, she pulled her arm out of his grasp.

"Look at you Nathan!" she continued. "Even now, you are blind drunk and violent! Once again, you have no respect for me nor the situation that we are in at the moment. All you can think of is yourself, your grievances, your ego! Leave me alone!"

As fast as she could, she walked away from him. She wanted to get out of there. She'd apologize to her client later and explain the state of emergency. She rushed out to her car.

To her horror, Nathan stood next to it, waiting for her.

Faithless Romance

How did he manage to get here so fast?

"Claire, I'm sorry," he said, trying to prevent her from getting into her car. "Forget what I said earlier, I didn't mean it. You are right, I'm drunk! I miss you, Claire. I'm serious! Let me make it up to you. Tomorrow, when I'm sober. I promise you I will be a gentleman. Let's share lunch together and talk it over. Give me another chance, please?" His bright blue eyes pleaded with her. He appeared mournful and genuine.

She sighed, not sure how to react to this latest fish tale. She fumbled with her car keys.

"Oh, alright then!" She gave in to get rid of him, aghast with her own decision. "We can meet up tomorrow, but the minute I smell booze on you, I'm out!" She threw him a stern look.

He smiled his sweetest smile when he replied, "thank you, my dear, thank you! I will not disappoint you this time! I guarantee you!" He tried to kiss her on the mouth but she held it off.

"We'll see," she replied. "Meet me at noon, at the Pink Salt restaurant and don't make me regret it, Nathan, I warn you!"

"I'll be a brave boy!" he taunted.

Without taking any further notice of him, she pushed passed him, started the engine and drove off.

A few blocks later, she stopped the car. She trembled, all shaken up by the confrontation. She needed a couple of minutes to compose herself.

What on earth happened just now? Why did I accept his request for reconciliation? I think I'm going to be sick!

Faithless Romance

She wanted to leave the olden days behind her but for some inopportune reason, it hit her right in the face again.

Tomorrow I will cancel the appointment, or maybe not? She hunched forward with her head against the steering wheel. She sighed, desperate and unsettled.

A complicated situation that she wished to avoid. "Why can't he leave me alone?" she moaned.

She couldn't deny it, it flattered her that he tried to win her back.

"Shucks, why does he have to look so athletic and robust?" she muttered, "and yet, so frail, so sad?" She was at a wit's end.

Men remained her biggest weakness, especially when they made advances. She knew it, yet she couldn't resist her urge to give them what they desired most.

The decision would be so much easier if she'd been back with Mason. Or if she had another steady boyfriend. But no, none of that. She got herself in hot water again!

Chapter 13

That night, Claire tossed and turned in bed. She mulled over her decision to accept Nathan's invitation. It became impossible for her to fall asleep. At five in the morning, she poured herself a cup of coffee.
Seated at the kitchen table, she stared at the mug with the black liquid in front of her. She put her hands around the warming porcelain.
Another two hours and she had to get ready for work. Not something she looked forward to today. These latest developments forced her to deviate from her daily routine. She had to determine whether she wanted to continue with their renewed contact. Before she organized her daily chores. Otherwise, it broke her concentration on the tasks ahead.
She wished she hadn't agreed on meeting Nathan for lunch, it only made things problematic. Was he genuine in his promise to change for her? She wanted to believe him and give him another chance. If only because she knew what it meant to be irresponsible. She had enough experience in that field. She understood his hurt, even though he brought it upon himself.
With a sigh of despair, she sipped at the black caffeine.
For a moment, she considered calling her sister Caroline in Spain, but what good would that do? She guessed her reaction beforehand. "Claire, it's obvious! You made a mess of your life! Grow up! Be a responsible woman. Find yourself a man who can give you everything you need!"

Well, that turned out to be unachievable! So far, she didn't have much luck in that field and she figured she tried her best to make it work.

She remembered the conversation that she had with herself years ago. Whether she should commit herself or whether to stay as free as a butterfly, fluttering around all day. She still didn't have the answer.

But, she longed for a solid relationship. With a man who understood her needs and her fluttery behavior. A solid rock, readjusting the continuous movement of the ocean water.

She finished her coffee and took a long shower to refresh her sleep deprived body and soul. The warm water soothed her skin and she let the jet stream of the shower head run over her face and washed her hair.

She hummed her favorite song, "Somewhere Over The Rainbow". And once she dried herself off with a large, soft bath towel, she got dressed. She decided to wear a white trouser suit with a lilac blouse. Meanwhile, the yes or no struggle continued in her head.

When she opened the curtains, it turned out to be a gorgeous sunny day. At long last, she decided to give Nathan another chance. She could, at least, listen to what he had to say. First, though, duty called, and she went to work, where she soon got caught up in management meetings and budget approvals.

At one pm she left the office for her appointment with Nathan.

She arrived late, on purpose, to make him suffer and let him speculate whether she'd show up or not.

Faithless Romance

Or, maybe he got cold feet and he changed his mind. Another reason to review her decision before she let him back into her life again.

When she stepped into the restaurant, she didn't have to wait long to find out whether he kept his word or not. Straight away he announced his presence and he walked up to her.

"Hello, Claire! I'm so glad you came!" he said, "I worried you wouldn't show up. You look most amazing! Is that a new suit?" He looked down and up her body and his eyes spoke volumes.

He sure knows how to flatter a woman, she noticed with sarcasm. And it works, even with me! I'm still falling for his charms, no matter what!

He led her to their table, and he placed a chair beneath her for her to sit down. For a stupid reason, her nerves got the better of her. She watched him with scrutinizing eyes. He still resembled a Greek God, she decided. No wonder he has this power over me!

She began to look over the lunch menu, to avoid any further amorous appreciation.

"Can I get you a white wine?" he asked her, "your favorite, a Sauvignon Blanc?"

"That sounds lovely, thank you," she replied, "and you can order me the Waldorf salad while you're at it."

"An excellent choice," he buttered her up. "I will have the salmon."

"And you said you were broke?" she reminded him.

She saw that she brought him embarrassment and she sympathized with him.

Faithless Romance   68

"Don't worry, though," she added. "I'll put it on our company's representation costs as a business luncheon."

"What a great idea!" he responded, with relief. "In that case, I can order a whole bottle of wine!"

"Don't push your luck, Nathan!" she warned him. "There's no need to overspend business funds!"

"You're right, of course, my apologies! I was only joking!" he tried to cover up his brutal suggestion.

He gazed at her with his gorgeous blue eyes. "I forgot how beautiful you are Claire!" He drooled all over her.

"You didn't deserve my atrocious treatment. I'm an absolute idiot for having done so. Can you forgive me?" He tried to touch her hands, but she withdrew them in a flash.

"Well, to be honest, Nathan, I can't say. How can I be sure you won't relapse into the same habits again?" She sounded harsh.

"Are you willing to give up on your outside activities?" she asked him with a stern face.

He moved back and forth in his chair. Careful with his response.

"The thing is," he began. "I finished with most of them. But only because I haven't got the money for it anymore. Yet, besides that, I'm willing to stay home more, if that makes you happy!"

It sounded unconvincing. And she wondered whether he'd fall back to his old habits once he had a filled bank account again. For now, though, she didn't have to worry.

"Are you confident you will find another job?" she confronted him, knowing it to be a sensitive issue.

Faithless Romance

"As a matter of fact I have one lined up," he admitted. He kept his calm even though tension showed.

"It wasn't easy to find one because of my last reference." He gave her a stern meaningful look. "But Coopers & Co are willing to give me another chance. On the condition that I follow an anger management course. And of course, I will accept."

So he will soon have money again, she worried. But, she put it aside and said, "I'm impressed, good for you! And don't forget to drink less alcohol!" she warned him with a grin on her face.

Before he could reply, their food arrived, and they started their meal.

"The food is delicious here," she commented.

"It sure is," he agreed.

"Claire, did you reflect on what I said last night? I mean, I'm so sorry for what I did and how I behaved. When I said I wanted us to try again, I meant it! Despite your lack of confidence in me! We should be able to make it work this time. After all, we came to the other side of the world together. To start afresh. We shouldn't blow our happiness because of a few minor disagreements!"

"Minor disagreements!" she hissed. "Nathan, I'd not call them minor if I were you. To me, they were major issues! You're not getting away with it. It's not that easy!"

"Alright, alright, I'm sorry," he was quick to respond.

"Of course, they were important to you! Forget what I just said." He reached for his glass of red wine and to her disgust, he emptied it in one go.

"I tell you what," he continued.

"Why don't I stay at your place for a couple of days and we'll see what happens. We can't reconcile our differences during one lunch date, now can we? It is far too complicated for that. What do you say?"

Uneasy and apprehensive, he waited for her reaction.

She didn't answer straight away, overwhelmed by this sudden proposition. And not keen on the idea. But, she wanted to give him an opening, for reasons beyond her own logic. She put aside her hesitations.

"Fine," she said. "You can come over this weekend and we'll see how it goes."

He threw a hand kiss at her across the table.

"You won't regret it my darling, you won't."

"Let's hope so," she replied, distant and cool. She glanced at her watch. "I have to dash off now, duty is calling."

She paid the bill and hurried away, not giving him the opportunity to kiss her goodbye.

This face-off could be the biggest one yet to come, with Nathan staying over. Though this time, he lodged in her house, which she paid for. If she didn't agree with his attitude, she'd throw him out!

Chapter 14

More than once, she wanted to call it off. The prospect of a challenge excited her. But she doubted her own sanity over their compromise. Nathan wasn't that trustworthy. What if he drank too much again? She couldn't bare having a drunkard around her.
"Stop being such a wimp," she told herself. "You don't know and there's no point in worrying in advance."
That next Saturday, Nathan stood in her kitchen, washing the dishes even though she had a dishwasher. He insisted on doing it, just as he insisted helping her with other household chores. He brought her breakfast in bed. They walked along the beach together. And during the evening he sat next to her, watching television in silence. Now and then he asked her whether he could get her something.
He avoided drinking any alcohol and she understood that wasn't easy for him. She noticed how his hands trembled and it was obvious he had withdrawal symptoms.
He committed himself to serve her. To show his best side. His new job didn't start for another month. Since he had to move out of their earlier apartment, she allowed him to stay with her for a while.
One morning he stood in the shower and she needed her body lotion out of the bathroom cabinet.
She saw his silhouette through the shower door. His strong, masculine build, which she admired and remembered so well.
The lack of sexual activity and the sight of his naked body made hers respond.

A familiar sensation rose from her toes towards her neck.

"Is that you Claire?" he asked, aware of her presence. "Can you hand me the towel, please?" He opened the door and now stood naked in front of her. Her heart pounded and her entire body inflamed when he came closer. In an impulse, he pulled her against his wet chest.

"You want me!" he said in a husky voice. "Admit it, Claire! There has always been an amazing sexual attraction between us. Let's make love, for old time's sake!" He pulled her even closer towards him. He pressed his lips against hers, strong and demanding, not waiting for an answer.

She loved his strength, his dominance to make her want him. She surrendered to the lustful sensation and enjoyed every single minute of it.

They moved from the bathroom to the bedroom. Their bodies moved as one. And at the height of their lovemaking, she moaned out loud. "Nathan! Oh yes! Nathan!"

Afterward, they lay in silence next to each other for a while, each letting sink in what just happened. Even though the intimacy elated her, this unexpected turn in their revived relationship baffled her. Was this worth a new future with him or just a temporary satisfaction of her own needs? A question only she herself could answer. She needed time to think.

Nathan broke the romantic spell by getting out of bed. She watched him when he got dressed.

"I think I'll go out for a walk," he announced, with a dismal gloom on his face.

A queer and unfamiliar expression. After a brief kiss on her mouth, he left without saying another word.

What was that? she wondered, by now somewhat recovered from the overwhelming affinity. Is he as confused as I am? Does he have second thoughts?

A riddle, difficult to guess. She took a quick shower, meanwhile gathering her own thoughts. Until now he kept his promise. He showed kindness, support, and attentiveness, everything a woman wanted.

Soon he'd have a job again and things were looking encouraging. She considered the possibility to become a couple again. Yet doubts remained in the back of her mind. But, when Nathan returned, everything became clear to her.

"Ah! There she is!" he spoke loud-voiced with a double tongue. "The lady-in-waiting, waiting for her knight in shining armor!" He swayed towards her.

"And here I am!" He pulled her over with force and shoved his hips against hers with such violence that it hurt her.

"You idiot!" she shouted at him, "you've been drinking again!" In response, he grabbed her by her hair and jerked her face towards his upon which he kissed her in a vicious manner. She loved his strength, but this went too far! His behavior was altogether barbaric!

She fought back and she yelled at him again, this time in pain. "Nathan, stop! You're crazy! Nathan!"

"Yes! Fight me, vixen!" he laughed loud and hysterical. "Make me fight for it. Let me conquer you!"

His drunken laughter kept filling the room when he slapped her in the face.

"Come here bitch!" he commanded. "Enough of this! Do what you're supposed to do! Please your man! I want it!"

His grip on her became even tighter and Claire now became most frightened. He'd gone insane! His grasp altered, it became stronger than usual and there was no reasoning with him.

She panicked and the adrenaline in her body put her in survival mode. With strength beyond her own imagination, she succeeded to free herself from his headlock.

"Get out!" she shouted berserk, "get out! Before I kill you!" She pushed him towards the front door. And before she realized what and how it happened, he stood outside and she slammed the door in his face.

Her whole body shivered. In a frenzy, she gathered his belongings. She behaved on autopilot. She threw his stuff out of the window.

"Leave!" she yelled at him, "leave now or I call the police!" She hurried back to the living room, and she collapsed on the sofa. She cried and cried and cried.

How long she'd sat there, she didn't know. After a while, she calmed down. She walked around the house like a zombie, not knowing what to do or where to go next.

Unexpected, her long lost feelings for Mason emerged.

She missed him more than ever and she wished wholeheartedly that she'd never treated him the way she did. She wished him to be there, to comfort her.

But he wasn't, and she had to get a hold of herself.

Faithless Romance

The next day she called in sick at the office. She stayed in bed the entire day, eating ice cream and chocolates and brood over her life and future. Do I have to talk to a shrink? she thought wretched, I need solid advice about my state of mind, that's for sure!

Chapter 15

Three days later, Claire went back to work. It drove her crazy to sit at home alone. But what happened with Nathan and his sexual assault, plagued her.

Still depressed, she found it difficult to concentrate at the office. At home, she neglected her household chores. In fact, she didn't want to do anything!

After a long inner debate, she decided not to seek the help of a psychiatrist. She hated the endless sessions, talking about her personal life and anxieties. It only made matters worse.

She blamed herself for what happened. Part of it because of her youth. During her college years, plenty of boys chased her, because of her good looks and popularity. Her first sexual experience was at the age of sixteen. And from then on she had plenty of short-term relationships. Every three months a new boyfriend. Whenever she met a man, she flirted with him until she got what she wanted. This time, though, it backfired on her, big time!

Rick called her twice. She explained what happened and asked him to leave her alone for a while. He understood, and she heard no more from him.

A friend and colleague, Sue Walker, came around one Saturday. Claire still walked around in her pajamas.

"Why don't you get dressed and we'll go for a walk along the beach?" Sue suggested.

"There's a gentle breeze blowing and the fresh air and the sounds and smell of the sea may cheer you up!

You don't need to dress up, just put on a tracksuit."

Claire laughed at this practical advice from her friend.

"All right, I'll do it, for you," she conceded, "since you insist."

Slow and reluctant, she got up. She took a brief shower and dressed in her favorite blue jogging pants and white shirt. The change into the casual outfit lifted her up.

When they walked along the shore, she took deep breaths. She inhaled the salty air while she listened to the sounds of the waves rolling in.

"You were right Sue, it's good to be outside, thanks."

"You're welcome," she replied, "that's what friends are for, isn't it?"

"I may be pregnant," Claire blurted out, unforeseen.

"What?" Sue responded and stopped in her tracks. "Are you sure? And is it Rick's or Nathan's?"

"No, I'm not sure, but I skipped my periods for two months and yes, it would be Nathan's. My guess is I got impregnated just before I first left him. I never had intimacy with Rick."

"Did you take a pregnancy test?" Sue asked.

"No, not yet. I'm afraid to do so. Besides, they are not always reliable."

"Well, most of the time they are," Sue replied, "but I would go see a doctor if I were you. You can also get an abortion you know if you explain the circumstances."

"Yes, I thought about that," Claire responded, "but I don't think I can do it. It's a baby, a small human being growing inside me," she said looking thoughtful.

"Visit your doctor!" Sue urged.

"I guess you're right. Will you come with me?"

Faithless Romance

"Of course, I come with you. Make an appointment first thing on Monday. Call me when he's available."

"Thanks, Sue, you're the best," she hugged her friend.

"Thanks for being there for me. Will you join me for an Italian ice cream at Leonardo's?" A spontaneous giggle burst from both of them.

When they returned from their outing, Sue left. Claire stayed alone with her thoughts again. The prospect of having Nathan's child became most daunting. She prayed for it not to be the case. That it was a false alarm. But Sue was right, she had to be sure!

On Monday, she called the doctor. His assistant scheduled an appointment for her that late afternoon. And asked if she'd bring in a urine sample in the morning. As promised, Sue went along for moral support.

"Miss Attaway, please sit down," Dr. Andrew Scott invited her. And you are?" He looked at Sue.

"Sue Walker, a close friend," she replied. "And we're not lovers," Claire added to the conversation.

Andrew Scott laughed in a kind way at that remark.

"Thank you for the information," he said. "But that's alright. There's no need to tell me."

Claire looked at him with interest. She had never met him before and he was rather handsome.

"Stop it, Claire," she warned herself, "don't do this!"

"Now, I'm afraid you're not pregnant, Claire," he announced.

She let a huge sigh of relief and replied, "thank goodness for that!"

"Ah! I take it you wouldn't be happy having a child?" he asked mindful and interested.

"No, not at the moment," she said firm and unshaken. "That much is certain! Later perhaps and with the right person, but not now."

"I see," he answered and looked at her more intense. "Do you worry a lot? Or are you depressed? Because that may cause your monthly periods to stop. Stress can be a strong factor in such cases."

"Yes, I suppose I am," she admitted.

Sue elbowed her and signaled her to tell him more.

She explained the situation.

"No wonder!" he concluded. "I will prescribe you a remedy that may help you overcome it," he proceeded. "And go for a long walk each day. Enjoy your surroundings. Perhaps your friend here can join you?" He looked at Sue in anticipation.

"Sure doc," she replied and smiled, "I'll be happy to."

"Good, then that's settled. Come back in about a month's time, to monitor your improvement. But contact me before that if needed."

Both women nodded their head in agreement and they left.

"That was a huge load off my mind," Claire said once they were outside.

"I'm so happy it turned out to be a false alarm!"

"I'm pleased for you," Sue replied comforting and glad.

"I hope the pills work for you. And you should ask for a transfer back to London. Even though I will miss you. Leave this life here behind. Catch up with Mason. You both need each other.

This Emily doesn't sound like the right person for him. Fight for him Claire, fight for him!"

Claire stood in front of her and replied in a soft voice. "Yes, I should, shouldn't I? The problem is that I never had to fight for any man, they always approached me. Mason did, be it in different circumstances and I ruined it. He is the only cure for me, the only person with whom I can share a meaningful relationship. My love for Nathan was irrational and wrong. I mislead myself. Mason is also mistaken about his love for Emily. I'm sure that deep inside his heart, he still longs for me. Thanks, Sue, for pointing it out once more. You are such a great support."

"Consider it, Claire. I'm serious! See you tomorrow at work!"

That evening she deliberated upon all her options. And she concluded that she wanted and needed to go back to London. She could ask for a transfer through her boss and she was hopeful he would grant her that. Then maybe, after a while, she'd be ready to face Mason. She hoped to make amends somehow.

Chapter 16

Claire's departure to Australia left Mason empty, sad, and lonely. It took several months to come to terms with her departure. Desperate to come to terms with his grief over her leaving he put his energy in running his jewelry store and franchise business.

She had taken up legal action against him, and demanded a share in his fortune. Fair enough and understandable. Since she helped him grow his business. He hired one of the best lawyers and left it to him to sort it out.

An opportunity arose to take part in a fashion and accessories expo, open to the public.

The time had come, to present his business there. Since Claire no longer handled that side of the enterprise, it needed a boost and exposure. He missed her drive and her enthusiasm.

During the retailers only session, a beginning jewelry designer approached him.

"Good afternoon, Sir," she said, polite and modest. "Is it all right if I show you my work?"

Her short blond hair and the serene, soft aura that surrounded her, captivated him. He figured she was in her early thirties. Her voice sounded warm, with a slight Irish accent.

"Yes," he answered with interest. "I'm always appreciative of new talent!"

Her designs were amazing! But she appeared insecure about her own work.

And yet, she'd been bold enough to introduce herself to him.

"Your style and creativity are unique!" he complimented her. "What is your name?"

"My name is Emily Summers. And thank you for the recognition!"

"You're welcome!" he responded. "Are you free for lunch? Then we can talk in more detail about your craft."

"Yes, I am!" she said, with a shy smile.

From then on, their relationship blossomed. It didn't take long for her to sway him.

He didn't want to make the same mistake. The one he made with Claire. Not to go anywhere! So, he spent as much time with Emily as possible! Because he wished for someone in his life. A spouse to love, and to share precious moments together. They enjoyed picnics in the park, sightseeing tours, visiting a museum, art galleries and shared other interesting activities.

In many ways, Emily differed from Claire, but they made a connection. His heart began to heal. He allowed for another chance to happiness in his life. Fate had turned in his favor and threw them together.

He introduced her designs to his business and sold the special editions in his shops. They were a huge success!

He instructed his lawyer to speed up and settle the deal with Claire. To give her what she wanted. And after eleven months, Emily Summers became his wife.

They had a small, simple wedding ceremony. No reception, and no dinner. Just the two of them and two witnesses. They needed nothing else.

Their togetherness was all that mattered to them.

But soon their bliss came to an end. They wanted to start a family, to have children. But, they failed to be successful.

After many visits to specialists, it came to light that Emily had ovulation problems. It caused infertility. And none of the stimulating drugs that got prescribed worked.

It shattered their dreams and Emily struggled to cope with this mortifying outcome. She lapsed into a deep depression.

It meant the beginning of another most strenuous period in Mason's troublesome life.

Why is this happening to me? he wondered. I don't deserve this! Why can't I live a happy life? As so many other people do? He suffered from his bad luck. But, he had to come to terms with his misfortune.

But, to watch his sweet Emily in such a dark place, became unbearable. He couldn't begin to imagine what was going on inside her head and why she didn't snap out of it.

After a while, he realized she needed professional help. With her mental suffering, and with her depressive state of mind.

One morning, she sat at the kitchen table. She looked miserable and fore-lorn. He took her hands and said: "my love, I understand that you're hurting. It's been difficult. For both of us. You're not getting any better. I can't bear to see you suffer, my dear Emily!"

He looked at her, she didn't respond.

"Do you wish to go on a short holiday?" he asked with forethought.

"Somewhere nice. Somewhere where they can help you get through this. I don't see what else there's left to do, darling. We've tried everything. This is our last chance to regain our happiness."

She looked so vulnerable, so fragile. She still didn't say a word. A hopeless case.

"Emily, please dear," he pleaded with her, "talk to me. Do you wish to take a short break away?"

Then, at last, she responded. Her eyes filled with tears when she spoke.

"I'm so sorry Mason," she said, while small water drops from her eyes, ran on her cheeks.

"It's such a mess. I'm so disappointed. It hurts, it hurts so much!"

He moved his chair closer and embraced her. "Of course it hurts, darling. Of course! But you shouldn't blame yourself. It's all right, we will get through this, I'm sure!" He kissed her tears away.

"I love you," she said and looked at him with sad eyes. "And maybe it is good for me to go away for a while," she continued. "But promise me you will not leave me there forever Mason, promise me, please!"

"I promise," he replied relieved. With the hope for her to get better.

The week following their decision, they drove to Chalton House. The convalescent home stood in the countryside of Aylesbury, only an hour drive from their home.

A stunning building with several out-houses or cottages in a breathtaking location. The perfect place to come to rest.

The team of specialists down there came well recommended and Mason put all his trust in them to cure Emily.

He promised to visit her every weekend. They allowed him to stay with her overnight on those occasions. To continue running his business during the week. And to make sure she got the love and attention she needed for her recovery.

It took several months of sessions with psychiatrists and art classes. At last, they reduced her anti-depressant medication. And she returned home.

Together they picked up the pieces and Emily worked on her designs again. She returned to her normal routines.

"Mason," she asked one evening. "I have an idea. What do you say if we adopt a needy child or two?" She looked at him with great anticipation.

"I've never considered that a possibility before," he admitted. "But because we both love to have children, it might be the answer to our prayers!" he added. He hugged her and kissed her on the cheek. "I tell you what! If you continue to be free from depression for the whole year, we will start the adoption procedure!" he agreed.

Yet, once more, their life turned into complete disorder. By another, unexpected and dangerous event.

It started a dreadful turning point in their relationship. Mason made the biggest mistake of his life, ever. When he followed a dangerous path to a disastrous destination.

His past came to haunt him and yet, in a way he was glad it caught up with him.

Even though his life with Emily had improved, he missed the passionate excitement he once shared with Claire. Something he'd given up hope for.

He just opened his main shop when the entry chime sounded. An early customer he presumed. He looked up from behind the counter and remained frozen to the spot.

That's impossible! He recollected his brains. Is that who I think it is? He didn't believe his own eyes!

Dressed in a casual outfit, blue jeans and a white embroidered blouse, stood Claire. The woman he tried to forget for so long! The one person he assumed to live on the other side of the world.

"Hello Mason," she said in her sweetest voice.

"I hope I didn't give you too much of a shock by turning up here, unannounced?"

"Of course, you did!" he murmured. "As if you don't know that!" He decided to play it cool and replied with calmness and restraint. "Well, in a way! From what I recall, you left the country, never to return!"

She walked towards him, in slow motion. She astounded him with her stunning looks and confidence. The refreshed acquaintance made his stomach turn and his heart pounded irregular and uncontrollable.

"Don't I get a welcome hug?" she defied him. "We shared so much together!"

He gave her a stern look, in an attempt to keep a distance between them.

"That's not a good idea, Claire! It's awkward enough already!"

She smiled a wry smile, disappointed that her call for affection remained unanswered.

"Fine!" she said, somewhat cranky. "Have it your way! How are things?" she then asked.

"Wonderful!" he replied, trying to stay cheerful. "I got married. Her name is Emily."

Claire remained unaffected by this announcement. "Yes, so I heard," she replied calm and unmoved. "Nathan and I broke up. Our relationship doomed to fail from the beginning," she added.

"I missed you, Mason. I wished we could have stayed together."

He cringed. How dare she do this to him? After the hurt, and the agony? She had the brutality to waltz into his life! To mess it up once more? It angered him, yet flattered him at the same time.

A most glamorous, and gorgeous woman, asked him to take her back. If he hadn't married Emily and if he didn't deem himself responsible for the fragile mental condition of his current wife, then he might have accepted Claire's plea. He still had strong feelings for her. But, not in the present circumstances! Not a chance!

"I understand it's difficult for you," she said, "now that you're married. But are you willing to have lunch with me today, for old times sake? To catch up, to forget and forgive the past?" Her dark fury eyes pleaded with him.

Much to his dismay, he heard himself accept her invitation. She charmed him and her bewitching powers were too strong for him to resist the temptation.

"I'm glad you will join me for a quick meal, thank you," she reacted in triumph. "We can meet at Charlie's again. I noticed his place is still there. Say around one pm?"

He nodded, unable to utter another word. At a loss and guilty. Left betrayed and confused.

"Good!" she grinned, turned her back on him and left him behind, in disarray.

He had to tell her this was the first and only time they'd meet. They shouldn't continue seeing each other.

Chapter 17

Claire was thrilled, despite the fact that Mason had given her the cold shoulder. He didn't convince her that he no longer had feelings for her. She still had emotional power over him. Otherwise, he wouldn't accept her invitation.
When she set eyes on him that morning, she had butterflies in her stomach and her knees were shaking. Confirming her strong longing for him. She wondered how long he'd be able to resist her flirtations. The undeniable mutual physical attraction between them never ceased to exist.
Closer to lunchtime, she waited in nervous suspense for his arrival at Charlie's. She'd booked the same table that they shared when they first got together. This time, she made sure she was seated before he arrived.
As she expected he came at one sharp. A waiter brought him to her and when he saw her, he greeted her composed. He tried to keep a distance, but at the same time, he couldn't hide his feelings for her.
"I'm so glad you came," she said. "I do appreciate it! It must be difficult for you and you have to believe me when I say that the same goes for me." She smiled at him and continued. "We both have been through a lot and I know you started a new life with Emily, but I also heard it has been burdensome. I'm so sorry, Mason."
"Yes," he admitted, somewhat reluctant. "It was problematic at times. I'm not sure what is worse, what you did to me or what I've experienced with Emily, to be honest."

Faithless Romance

"I guess I had that coming," she responded in all earnest.
"And I have been such a fool to hurt you the way I did," she confessed. "It wasn't worth betraying you the way I have and in the end, I got what I deserved. Nathan turned out to be a repulsive, disturbed, drunk!"
"It was that bad, was it?" he gathered. "I guess we both went through trials and tribulations," he added with a sad face. "But, it's too late now to turn back the clock!" he continued. "Emily needs me more than ever!"
He looked at her with dark, sorrowful eyes.
Claire swallowed hard when she heard him say the dreaded words, but she wasn't about to give up.
"I quite understand," she replied forgiving and she put her hand on his. To her relief, he didn't pull away.
Their lunch arrived and they ate in silence. Both occupied with their own thoughts and memories.
"Would you like to go for a walk along the water?" she asked him when they finished eating. "We enjoyed it so much, the first time. Remember?" She almost begged him to say yes, with her eyes.
"Yes," he agreed, "but those were different times. On the other hand, I could use some fresh air so why not?"
She felt elated that he didn't refuse. When they walked alongside each other, her body responded to his closeness. Filling her with warmth and love.
"Why on earth did I leave this man years ago?" she wondered.
She walked closer to him, causing his body to touch hers. Her heart went berserk.

And then, unforeseen, he turned her around and kissed her with extreme passion and emotion.

"Claire, why are you doing this to me?" he whispered.

"I can't resist you. It's wrong, but I need you, I want you."

"Oh Mason," she replied with affection. "I missed you! And I need you too! Yes, it's wrong! But maybe we can find a way to make up for lost time, without hurting Emily."

"Yes," he sighed, "maybe we can."

From then on, they continued seeing each other on a regular basis. One thing led to another and before long, they had a secret love affair. They met up whenever they could, where ever they could, in motels and hotels, all over town. Claire accepted she played second fiddle to Mason. For now, she was content.

Lucky for them, Emily worked a lot from home and she started a new jewelry line. It kept her occupied for a long time. Oblivious to Claire's return and the secret rendezvous with her husband.

Until that one day! The day that she wanted to surprise Mason with a stunning new piece of jewelry which she designed especially for him.

She went to show it to him and arrived at his shop unannounced when Claire happened to be there. She and Mason let their guard down. When Emily set a foot in the office at the back of the store, she caught them both kissing each other. She screamed and ran off, disoriented and most upset.

Mason rushed after her. "Emily, stop! Emily! It is not what you think! Emily, please!"

Faithless Romance 92

But she didn't stop. She ran and ran until he lost sight of her. In the meantime, Claire caught up with him.

"I'm so sorry Mason!" she cried. "I'm so sorry she saw us!"

He turned around and slapped her in the face with his hand. "No you're not!" he yelled at her. "This is exactly what you wanted to happen, isn't it? And I fell for it! I'm an idiot! I let you do this to me, to Emily, to us! You're a trickster, a sorceress! Leave, now! I never, ever want to see you again!"

The awful, painful look on Emily's face hit him like a lightning bolt. It reminded him of her frailty, her sensitivity.

"What was I thinking? How could I do this to her? What happened to our plan to adopt children, to start a family? Our true happiness got destroyed because of my weakness! Because I didn't resist the passion and the cunningness of my former fiance!" He felt sick to the stomach and angry, so angry!

He rushed back to his shop without taking any further notice of Claire. He closed for the afternoon and hurried home, hoping he could salvage his marriage and love for Emily.

Chapter 18

When he arrived home, Mason was in for a shock.

He called Emily several times, looked in the different rooms, but there was no sign of her. Then he noticed the door of the main bathroom. It was closed. Unusual, since they always left it ajar when in use. He found the door locked from the inside. And he panicked.

"Emily!" he shouted, "are you in there? Emily!" There was no answer.

His heart pounded and sweat drops rippled down onto his forehead. He banged against the door with his fists.

"Emily!"

Then, he heard a faint noise, the sound of someone in pain.

"Oh my God! What have you done? What have I done?"

He grabbed a crowbar from the storage room and hurried to break the door open with brute force. Multiple scenarios ran through his mind. What would he find in there?

With no further hesitation, he placed the tool between the door and the frame. He moved the iron device back and forth. After what seemed like hours, the lock gave way and the door flew open.

The scene that unfolded before his eyes gruesome. Emily lay in the bath tub, in a pool of bloody water. She appeared lifeless.

"Emily, oh Emily!" he sobbed. "What have you done?"

He grabbed her under the arms to heave her out of the water. Then he saw the cuts on her wrists.

Without delay, he snatched two towels from the rack and wound them around the cut areas. He tied them into a knot as far as possible, before he continued with his rescue. That wasn't easy. Even though she appeared fragile, it still was a lot of dead weight to lift.

For a second, she opened her eyes. When she saw him, she fought against him.

"Leave me alone!" she shouted in a hoarse voice. "Let me go!"

"Emily, please!" he pleaded with her. "I'm so sorry for what I've done, honey! But please, please, don't do this! We will get through this! Please, let me help you!"

He got a reprieve when she fell back into unconsciousness.

After another attempt to pull her body out of the water, he succeeded. With care, he lay her on the small floor carpet. Then he called the emergency services.

During the wait for them, he sat down with Emily. He stroke her hair and kept the pressure on the towels to stop the bleeding. How pale she looked. She still had her clothes on. The wet fabric clung to her thin body. Her skeleton showed through. He decided not to change her clothes, afraid to make things worse.

When the ambulance personnel arrived, they attended to her wounds and well-being. They agreed to take her to St Catharine's hospital first. Later, they would transfer her to a rest home for renewed mental treatment.

Mason explained what had happened before the suicide attempt. The medics showed compassion. They understood the sensitivity of what had unfolded, and why.

Faithless Romance

"It's fine, Mr. Brannigan," they commented. "This is not the first time we've witnessed such circumstances! It can happen in any marriage or relationship. We're only human! And some people are more sensitive than others. Each of us deals with adversities in different ways.

It is unfortunate that your wife wasn't strong enough to cope with your argument in a less dramatic way. Most unfortunate. It's obvious she needs help and we hope for your sake and her own that she will learn to be more rational."

Mason watched how his spouse got carried away on a stretcher. They sedated her so she wouldn't cause any harm during the ride to the hospital.

"It's better you don't visit her during the first two days," the men advised him. "And before you do, call the hospital first to inquire about her mental stability. If she's not ready to receive you, wait a while longer."

He nodded in agreement.

The ambulance drove off and Emily had gone away from him once more.

"Damn you, Claire!" he uttered. "Why did you have to come back? Why did you have to mess up our lives again?"

He went back inside and poured himself a large glass of bourbon. The clean up of the bathroom could wait. This new development required deliberation.

Two important women in his life! Out of his reach, each for a different reason.

The worst part of it was they were both dear to his heart. Even though they were such opposite characters.

Faithless Romance

Confused, he stared into his glass.

Where to go from here?

After a few minutes, he finished his drink. He decided. Emily remained his first priority. Besides, he told Claire he never wanted to see her again! Whether she'd listen? He had his doubts. She offered stubborn resistance.

Chapter 19

A few days later, he called the hospital. He found out they transferred Emily to Chalton House for further psychological treatment. Then he contacted the reception desk at the House to book a room for himself in an outhouse of the clinic. He wanted to be with Emily, to help with her recovery, in any way.
Next, he called Tony Lobbit. A long-time friend and business associate. He asked him to take over his shop and other business commitments for as long as necessary.
With the formalities taken care off, he packed a small suitcase for himself and another for Emily. He packed her favorite clothes and toiletries. In some way or other, beneficial towards her healing process.
Later that day, he settled himself in a guest cottage at Chalton House. By now, his energy levels deteriorated. The emotions, and at the same time trying to organize his business responsibilities caught up with him.
His eyelids got heavy and he yawned. Time to go to bed! He slept through the night without interruption, until he woke up at dawn. Refreshed, he got out of bed.
Hopeful for the day, despite the disturbances of the previous week. He sat at the table and enjoyed his breakfast at 7 am. Scrambled eggs on toast and a great cup of coffee. He opened the window near the table to get fresh air. The different flowers in the garden expelled a diverse range of a lovely soft scent. The smell of the bouquet entered his room.
A variety of songbirds giving him a private serenade.

The natural mood-lifters made him smile even brighter.

He enjoyed this time of the day! It made him content and happy to have a room facing the delightful garden of the rest home.

He received the morning paper. For a while, he kept himself occupied digesting the local news and world events. When he finished reading, he got dressed for the day. His phone went and Dr. George Watson announced himself.

"Good morning, Mr. Brannigan! You slept well, I hope?" he asked. "You may see your wife for a few minutes. This afternoon, say around two? She's still sedated so expect little in speaking with her, but it may be good she sees you again. I will ask my assistant, Dr. Alfred Henry, to stand close by, and watch her reaction."

"Oh, that's wonderful!" Mason responded. "Thank you for that! Let's hope she stays calm."

"Yes," Dr. Watson replied, "it's better for everyone if she does!"

It meant he had the whole morning to himself. After a short walk through the amazing gardens, he sat down to read a book, to reset his mind.

He tried to concentrate on the story line of Ernest Hemingway's "The Old Man and the Sea". But, after two chapters, his mind wandered back in time. When he first set eyes on Emily.

An hour later, Nurse Jully, a 33-year-old, somewhat overweight woman of Indian origin, came round to see him. She pulled him out of the reminiscence.

"It's time for lunch Mr. Brannigan," she spoke in her usual soft voice. She stood waiting at the door for him to invite her into the room.

"Please come in Miss Jully," he said.

"Is everything all right?" she asked, concerned for his well-being. "You've had a few difficult days behind you and still more to come," she added.

"Thank you for asking, nurse Jully," Mason replied. "Yes, I'm fine, don't worry. I was just thinking of the time I first met my wife."

Nurse Jully smiled at him with sympathy. "That's lovely Mr. Brannigan, sometimes the past can help us heal."

"Yes, it will, and in a way it won't," he replied, reflective. "We shared wonderful moments together, but she's also a most sensitive and kind person. And, I disappointed her and caused her enormous grief."

He bit his lips from frustration when he thought about Claire. How she pulled the wool over his eyes. What a fool he had been to take that risk! To cause pain to Emily, resulting in her present neurosis.

He sighed, meanwhile looking at the mature gardens of the home again. He spotted a magpie in one of the large oak trees and his expression softened.

"It's such a shame that people whom you love always hurt you the most, isn't it Mr. Brannigan?" nurse Jully acknowledged from experience.

"I'm sorry you have been through such hardship.

But you said it. You've had many happy moments to look back at. Am I right?"

She looked at him, waiting for his response.

"Yes," he confided, "we share lovely memories!"

He took the tray with his lunch from her and put it on the coffee table.

"Well," nurse Jully said with a cheerful face. "You think of those special moments Mr. Brannigan. You'll be grateful, I'm sure of it!"

He turned around and eyed her, a wry smile twisting his lips when he answered, "I will, I will!"

Then there was silence. The nurse left the room, leaving him once again alone with his thoughts. He defied the advice he received and he continued to muse over the problematic years. His face saddened when his thoughts went back in time once more, to the months he spent with Claire.

How different his life could have been if he had met Emily way before he met Claire! That early morning, now six years ago. When he opened the doors of the jewelry store and saw a woman in distress. A gorgeous woman! Who searched for something.

Her auburn hair caught fire from the sun's rays shining on her. When she noticed his gaze, she looked up at him. He remembered a pair of intense black eyes. Sparkling diamonds embedded in an oval shaped, almond colored, most beautiful face he had ever seen. Her warm, broad smile that exposed well-maintained teeth. To melt any man's heart on the spot!

Dressed in an immaculate cream skirt and burgundy blouse. Both complemented her skin tone. She spoke like an angel when she asked for his help.

He fell in love with her, there and then.

His overzealous love for Claire made him blind.

Much too late he found out she wasn't ready for the commitment to marry him.

She wanted and tried to accept his wish for a married life and his affection towards her. But he came to realize that it suffocated her. He would lose her one day to someone else, no matter how hard he tried to meet her needs.

Their expanding and demanding business did little good to their relationship either. But there was no stopping.

He'd been thinking to sell part of his chain of stores. To get more spare time to enjoy a private life.

When he finished his lunch, he looked at the clock. It was time for his visit to Emily.

Chapter 20

When Mason shouted at her he never, ever, wanted to see her again, Claire faced the brutal realization she made her biggest mistake ever! One that left her devastated and guilt-ridden.

Back in her rental accommodation, she felt sick and not only because of what happened. A month ago, her worst fears got confirmed. She'd become pregnant. Now in her third month. With no doubts this time. The child had to be Mason's!

It frightened and upset her. What to do? Did he turn his back on her, for good? She wanted him to know! They had to restore their relationship! She refused to give in to defeat, determined to put things right.

I want to bear his child! She thought strong-minded. It's the only thing left of the love of my life, she decided. But before it comes to this world, I have to sort myself out so I can be a proper, loving parent. To be strong enough to present it to Mason one day. She couldn't bear the thought of her child not having a father.

She'd heard of the Healing Monastery House for Guests. They allowed single women to stay in retreat and receive guidance in challenging times. Maybe she had to adhere to their religious practice, but she figured that could be of use. They had 50 volunteer counselors available. Well trained professionals, who gave their time for free to offer support.

She could apply for a sabbatical year at work, allowing her to stay at the Abbey as long as was necessary.

She arranged to meet the Human Resource Manager of her employer. Then asked for a consultation with Father Martin at the Monastery.

Four days later, she had her talk with the pastor. She looked around the waiting room. A large space, with high ceilings and oak floors. A worn-down red and yellow Persian carpet lay underneath a robust oak coffee table.

The walls painted in a terracotta color. Decorated with ancient pictures of priests. A huge log fire dominated in the middle of the room. A brown leather sofa and two large leather chairs stood in front of it.

She also noticed a few antique lamps and religious ornaments. The atmosphere of Victorian times preserved and it looked impressive.

"Miss Attaway, welcome to our congregation," Father Martin welcomed her most friendly and serene. "I heard that you are with child! Such a precious gift to this world, and his!" He looked to the heavens.

His remark brought a faint smile to Claire's face. She'd only just stepped in and God was present.

"What can we do for you?" he asked.

"Well, I hope you can help me find peace of mind. And cure me of an everlasting hunger for sexual adventures," she said bold and decisive.

The clergyman looked displeased about her use of words, but she ignored it and went on with her plea.

"This baby here," she pointed at her belly, "is a result of true love, for a man I once intended to marry. But I betrayed him, not once, but twice," she confessed.

"And," she added, "I caused grievance to his new wife.

A woman with an already fragile state of mind. Because I couldn't control my strong erotic desire for men."

Her hormones were playing up, and she became tearful. She pressed her lips together, apprehensive for his response to these revelations.

"And?" he coaxed her to finish her story, instead of responding straight away. He handed her a tissue.

"And," she said, soft and sniveling. "I long to be with the father of my child. I believe we belong together. We both got lost in finding the right path to our mutual happiness. But, we do not wish to hurt the other woman," she completed her admission. There, she'd said it and it was the truth!

"Yes, problematic," the pastor said with empathy. "That sounds like a precarious status quo. I understand why you need help with such a delicate situation. You gain insight from counseling sessions," he derived. "I will discuss your circumstances with the supervisors, to come up with a schedule. And to decide which counselor best fits your profile." He paused for a moment.

"You are most welcome to stay in our House For Guests until and up to the birth of your child. I will have a room made ready." He rose from his chair and Claire followed suit.

"Thank you so much, Father," she responded, grateful for his positive decision.

"Don't thank me, my dear," he smiled, "thank the Lord for bringing you here to get the help you need."

Uncertain how to react to his suggestion, she kept quiet.

"I will be in touch with you soon," he said when they left the room. "Are you having a girl or a boy?" he asked, "and when is it due?"

"I don't know, yet. I'm having an ultrasound done next week." She caressed her belly gentle and tender. "Almost six months to go," she answered his other question.

"Let's pray to God your child will be healthy and happy," he finished.

"Yes, let's," she replied somewhat hesitant. She hurried away from the scene. "I better get used to that Christian stuff," she murmured. "If I want to become a new woman, I have to!" She sighed and drove back to her apartment, exhausted from the emotions.

After a short nap, she wrote an email to Leonardo, with whom she stayed in touch. She told him of her possible stay at the Monastery. She didn't tell him about her pregnancy, though, not yet.

When she received a reply from him, he told her that Emily's mental health had not improved. That Mason had to sell part of the business to be able to pay for her treatment. The future looked less promising than she hoped for. Lots to be done before she could start her new life.

And that became even more obvious when she fell for the charms of her new counselor at her first session.

His name was Felipe. Dark Hispanic features and a gorgeous accent. His skin tanned, his eyes and straight hair were an intense black. Well-built, with the most amazing broad smile.

He came well prepared, and he took the bull by the horn.

"It is nice to meet you, Claire," he began. "You're attracted to me, no? Your eyes betray you!"

She looked at him in amazement, at once flustered. He caught her on the spot.

"Wow! You are good!" she tried to explain it away. "I believe I've found my match!"

He roared with pleasure when he replied, "yes, you are right, I am the toreador and you are the bull! It will be my pleasure to tame you!"

He leaned forward and looked her straight in the eyes when he said; "not every man wants the same thing from you, Claire! For me, our sessions are professional. I'm married, and happy. You are carrying the child from a man you can't have."

"For now," she added, upset.

"Fine, for now," he agreed. "We have work to do, that much is clear! I understand your frustration and the need to feel wanted after the recent problems."

He fell backward in his chair and folded his hands behind his head.

"Bien, tell me your life's story," he invited her, "I'm listening."

She unraveled her past. Her complicated youth. The arguments with her sister Caroline. The attention the boys and later adult males gave her. The complications that followed. How she became more or less addicted to love and fluttered from one man to the next until she met Mason.

She explained her inner struggle to commit to him. Why she agreed to marry him.

How she fell back into her old habits and got what she deserved. Her eyes became watery when she finished.

"Mi Cara mia, I don't think you deserved that!" Felipe responded to her final conclusion. "You got confused! Deep inside you want to embrace marriage to your true love. But because of your past, you have been sabotaging your own happiness. Together we come to terms with that! And I make sure you are ready for the ultimate commitment, I promise!" He smiled at her and gave her a comforting look.

His professionalism and encouraging words reassured her. She made the right decision to enter the Monastery.

You will have a Daddy my little one, she thought sentimental and rubbed over her round tummy with her hands. I'm sure of that.

Felipe stood up. "This is all for today," he announced. "You must be tired."

She nodded in agreement.

"I will see you next week, same day, same time. "Take a rest, Claire," he proceeded.

"It will be good for you, and the baby! The library has plenty of interesting books to read, about marriage and parenthood. You can start with one of those."

"That sounds like a good idea," she replied, "thank you."

She left the room with mixed feelings.

Chapter 21

Mason went to the psychiatric wing of the center where a polite and friendly Dr. Henry greeted him.

"Good afternoon Mr. Brannigan! I hope you are settled in our guest cottage? Are you comfortable enough?"

"Yes, I am. The lodging is more than adequate, thank you," Mason replied, in a businesslike manner. "How is Emily?" He got to the point straight away.

The doctor smiled with empathy.

"It's still early days to say whether she will be all right or not," he responded. "We have given her a tranquilizer and the drug makes her dopey. But she may recognize you! I watch from a distance and observe her reaction when she does. Are you ready to visit her?"

"I sure am!" Mason confirmed. "In fact, I love to see her!"

"Right then," Dr. Henry replied. "Follow me, please."

They walked towards double glass doors and entered a middle size room. Inside stood four large armchairs and coffee table. In one chair sat his Emily. Her head dropped, her hands clenched together in her lap. She looked even worse than he'd imagined. He inhaled deep and heavy, twice. And tried to stabilize his nerves.

"I'll be in that corner," the doctor pointed out, and he walked away.

Somewhat apprehensive, Mason walked towards his wife.

He sat next to her and whispered, "hello darling, it's me, Mason. You look wonderful!"

She didn't respond.

He touched her blond hair, her hands, gentle and caring.

Without warning, she freaked out and screamed. She became wild and her movements uncontrolled! When she looked up at him, her eyes stood wide and deranged.

"You! You!" she shouted. "Go away! You are the devil! I don't want you here!" She flung out of the chair and she began hitting him. With such violence, that Dr. Henry had to interfere.

"Calm down, Emily," he urged her, "you're fine! Don't be afraid! You're safe! Everything is all right!"

She sobbed loud and disturbed and howled like a wolf.

"I think you better leave," the physician told Mason. "This is worse than I imagined. Far worse! The drugs weren't effective. I will speak to you later."

Mason nodded his head and left the room, shaken and mortified. What just happened? he thought, crushed.

What has become of you, Emily? Will you ever get over this? Oh, Emily, what did I do?

He went for a walk and sat on a garden bench, staring into nothing. He wept in silence until he had no more tears left. Three hours had past when he returned to the cottage. He poured himself his favorite whiskey. The personnel told him not to consume any alcohol, but he stashed a small bottle away in a secret place. He drank the scotch, but only one shot.

Darkness fell. Family and friends left the other inhabitants of the home to their own enclosed world.

In half an hour they brought him his supper.

Dr. Watson left a message on his phone, inviting him to a meeting the next morning at ten.

Sipping from his glass, he continued his journey on memory lane. A heartsick man. His sadness showed and engulfed him! He understood Emily's behavior, but she hurt him. Although he deserved her rejection. She had reason enough to hate him. Her present conduct was his own fault. Guilt ate him up inside. If only he could live those past years over again! Then he'd take a different approach!
A shuffling sound behind the entrance door of his cabin, startled him.
"Oh, no! I forgot! Time for my supper!" he uttered.
He took the last sip from his whiskey and rinsed the glass. Then pushed a peppermint in his mouth, to hide the smell of alcohol on his breath.
Miss Martha, one of the other nurses, came in to deliver his meal. A woman in her late twenties, most unpredictable mood-wise. But an expert on medicines and their side-effects.
She wished him good evening, placed the tray with food on the table and hurried out. Not in the mood, and no time to chat. Mason didn't mind.
Today's dinner, comprised of classic jacket potatoes with a herb on top, spinach, and a meatball. Simple but tasteful and healthy.
He sat at the small table near the window and ate. From time to time he looked at the tranquil and enchanting garden. The light of the small lanterns around the footpath created a romantic scenario. The window stood ajar, and he heard the relaxing sound of crickets.

His supper triggered the thought of Claire's awkward goodbye at the restaurant, at the beginning of their friendship. He remembered he lay low for a while, to assess her position. A most difficult decision and strenuous weeks. Unable to concentrate on his shop and his customers. Restless, and frustrated, he became eager to take firm action. To make her his wife.

He convinced himself that she tested him or she really was busy with her job, as she said. But, she pulled away from him. Yet he gave her the benefit of the doubt.

She'd come back to him if she was ready. And she did! With complications! Then the inevitable separation. But despite everything, she remained in his thoughts. If he stayed true to himself, he admitted he loved her. As much as he loved Emily, be it for different reasons.

Falling asleep that night became impossible.

The image of Emily's backlash at him that afternoon remained vivid. He couldn't let it go. But, he had to accept she lived in her own small world. She closed the door on him and left him helpless. Ironical, to say the least.

He didn't think Dr. Watson would bring good news tomorrow. Emily's healing process and recovery would be slow. Years, maybe.

Whether she ever wanted to share her life with him again? An important question, burning on his lips.

In fact, he wouldn't blame her if she left him forever!

Exhausted, he fell asleep at five in the morning. When nurse Jully knocked on the door at seven with his breakfast, he felt drained and miserable.

"Good morning Mr. Brannigan," she walked in, looking cheerful. "It's a bright and lovely day today. Did you sleep well?"

"No, I didn't," he replied stretching his aching body, yawning loud and broad. "I think I might need a nap later on."

She exchanged an understanding look with him.

"That's such a pity, sorry to hear that," she said. "Don't you worry, your wife is in good hands!"

He smiled, but only just. "Of course, nurse Jully," he responded in earnest, "but I just can't help myself."

She positioned the tray with scrambled eggs, toast, and marmalade and poured him a cup of coffee. "Perhaps you feel better after a cuppa," she reasoned.

"Enjoy your breakfast, Mr. Brannigan! I hope your day turns out to be a good one!" She left him to his own devices.

He opened the windows and inhaled the fresh morning air. As usual, the flowers emitted an odor, entering the room.

Birds sang and the morning sky turned scarlet red. An amazing sunrise! It promised to be a lovely day.

After breakfast, he felt somewhat refreshed, even more so when he had taken a shower.

He dressed in summer pants and a short-sleeve shirt for the day. Time to go and see Dr. Watson.

The psychiatrist stood tall in his office.

A luxurious and sophisticated space. Lined with wood panels. He gazed out of the window when Mason entered.

He turned around when he became aware of his visitor.

"Ah! Mr. Brannigan! There you are!

Good morning, please take a seat."

Mason seated himself on one of the brown leather Chesterfield chairs. Meanwhile, the specialist went through the paperwork on his desk.

"Yes, here!" he announced. "The form I need you to sign. Let me explain a few things to you," he continued.

"Dr. Henry told me about the unfortunate incident yesterday. We both concluded that your wife suffers from a severe psychoneurosis. She's in a most unhappy place. She has strong feelings of anxiety, obsessional thoughts and plenty of insecurities. We need a multifaceted approach as in medication and psychotherapy. It can take more than a year for her to recover if she recuperates!" he frowned. He looked Mason straight in the eyes.

"Because of her history of depression, and considering what you both have been through!" he continued. "That you couldn't have any children! The confrontation with your ex-wife! It will be a long and strenuous process for her."

"You've just confirmed my worst fears," Mason replied, dismal.

"I can't even imagine what goes on in her head. Please do whatever it takes to make life bearable for her again, Dr. Watson. Whatever it takes!"

"Of course, Mr. Brannigan! We will do whatever is in our power to cure your wife. I need you to sign this form. In which you agree with the proposed treatments. And her stay with us, for how long it takes, to improve her health."

He handed the document to Mason.

"Take your time to read it through, and once you've signed, you can leave it with my secretary," he finished. "You must excuse me, I need to do my rounds."

He tapped Mason on the shoulder.

"Your wife receives the best care we can offer her. She gets the attention and therapy she requires. It's better you don't visit her, for a while," he added.

"There's nothing more you can do than to return to your daily business affairs. I will let you know when she's ready to receive you."

"Thank you, Dr. Watson, I guess you're right. I trust your professional judgment."

Mason left with a heavy heart and a thousand thoughts on his mind. Once again, his life got turned upside down.

He had to sell part of his enterprise. Not only to have more tranquility in his life but to pay the huge bill for Emily's treatment.

He'd speak with Tony.

Chapter 22

Claire lived in a simple room in the House For Guests. With a single bed, a bedside table, a small dining table, two chairs and a wardrobe. All made from the same, dark oak wood. Next to the bed stood a small bedside lamp. A white pendant lamp hung from the ceiling.

The monks required silence and enclosure, so most of the time, it got quiet around her. Difficult for her in the beginning, coming from a hectic office environment. But, a welcome reprieve to cope with the ups and downs of her pregnancy.

Felipe made her read several self-help books. In their counseling sessions, he gave her leads and guidelines to stay on track. And ways to improve her emotional sensibility towards men. During the next few weeks, she learned to accept her own character flaws, and how to avoid making the same mistakes.

The ultrasound showed she carried a boy inside her. Now and then he kicked. She read books about parenthood and raising a child, and got more self-assured. Looking to reach her goal of becoming a caring and responsible mother.

Mason stayed around in her mind. Not a day passed by without her thinking of him. She wondered how things were with him and Emily. Did she have to stay in a mental institution for the rest of her life?

If the latter is the case, it's easier for Mason to see his son, she figured. She let out a heavy sigh.

That part of her life remained problematic, and she wasn't sure how to handle it.

Thus, it came as a shock, and as a relief, when she received the email from Leonardo. He told her that Emily committed suicide. The funeral to be held in two days time, at Abney Park.

Even though Emily's death made matters easier, it didn't make matters less complicated. Emily meant the world to Mason. She had to allow him to grief over her death. But, she had a sparkle of hope it re-opened the door for herself. When he learned that she bore his child things could turn around! From the beginning, he wanted to have children. A faint smile formed around her mouth.

At her next meeting with Felipe, she told him the news.

"Do you feel responsible for Emily's death?" he asked her.

"Yes, in a way I do," she admitted. "If I hadn't returned from Australia and if I hadn't wooed Mason the way I did, she might still be alive today." Her own words hit home.

"Then I must tell you that you are wrong, Cara Mia," he said in a serious undertone.

"From what you told me, she was an over-sensitive and mentally unstable person. And if it wasn't for you, I'm sure there would have been another strong reason for her to take her own life. Because she didn't give her husband the children he wanted."

"Yes, but they would adopt," Claire defended her.

"For a woman like Emily, that's not enough. Trust me, Claire, this was bound to happen, sooner or later," he spoke in a firm tone.

"I guess you are right Felipe," she conceded. "Emily didn't have the strength to cope with her shortcomings. It is sad, and Mason must be gutted!" She looked out the window onto the parking lot.
"Will he forgive me, and let me back into his life?" she asked her mentor, looking hopeful.
"Over time, that might be possible Claire. You said yourself that he loves you and that he chose her because of her circumstances. But now she's gone, he may let you into his life once more. Give him time to heal. Wait until your boy is born, that's only two months away. The birth will ask energy from you. Once you've given birth, you can write him a letter. Who knows, he may need you then, more than ever. It's the start of a new future for the both of you, and your son."
He smiled at her and asked, "have you decided on a name for your child yet?"
"Matthew," she replied in a warm, happy voice. "His name is Matthew, after Mason's father."
"That's wonderful Claire," Felipe responded with delight. "What a lovely thing to do! I'm sure he will be most grateful to you. It's a special token of your love for him. Well done!"
His words pleased her, and she was content.
She died to tell Mason about their child.
After all the fallacies, she wanted a reconciliation. To undo the past, and to lay the foundation for a better future! If he loved her as much as she thought he did, he'd give her a chance!

She wished to go to Emily's funeral, but she didn't dare attend!
On the day, she watched the burial in secret, from behind a tree at the cemetery.

Chapter 23

Mason struggled to come to terms with the intense traumatic event of Emily's suicide. Earlier that day when he arrived at the clinic to spend the weekend, she had improved.

Then panic broke loose throughout the clinic. Alarms sounded and personnel ran backward and forwards.

Since no one came for him, he decided to stay put. In the case of a fire or other serious incident, they would notify him, he reasoned. And, they did.

But instead, he received the devastating news! Emily took her own life. She used the sheets of her bed to hang herself. A complete riddle! The event even dumbfounded and embarrassed Dr. Watson.

"I'm so sorry for your loss Mr. Brannigan!" the nurse said, looking at him in anticipation. She lingered, waiting for a response to the gruesome news he received.

"Thank you, Miss Martha," Mason replied, in a business-like manner. "Emily said farewell, in her own peculiar way," he finished. Tears welled up in his eyes. He turned around to hide his sorrow.

"Right, I leave you alone then," she decided. The door closed behind him.

How is this possible? He asked himself, as he returned to his favorite chair near the window. Why wasn't she strong enough? Why didn't she allow me to help her one last time?

Anger rose towards Claire. How could she! How could she do this!

He stared out the window of his cottage at Chalton House. In the garden, residents enjoyed the company of their children and grandchildren. A warm and pleasant evening. The air filled with laughter, but not for him.

He sat in silence, somber and desolated. His hands trembled when he tried to come to terms with what he lost.

If only he had listened to his instincts! Now he lost the two most important people in his life! His mouth twisted into a bitter smile. His face softened when he recited a poem he wrote for Emily when they first met. How special that period had been! Too much to handle!

"I will stay here for a few months and get therapy myself. I need help to come to term with my grief!"

He continued with his reminiscence. His mind reflected on the years with Emily. She would still be alive today if he had met her way first. Before he set eyes on Claire! Poor Emily, such a warmhearted, caring person, who had loved him with all her heart and soul. She deserved the most gracious funeral.

I hope the service companies open on Saturday, he worried. So I can arrange everything. He grabbed his coat and went outside.

"I want a drink," he muttered, "this time from the nearest pub!"

After a few glasses of bourbon, it didn't take him long to fall asleep that night.

The next morning he woke up with a strong headache.

He asked nurse Jully to bring him a few aspirins with his breakfast. When she arrived, she looked concerned.

Faithless Romance

"Are you sure you are all right Mr. Brannigan?" she asked. She gave him an investigating look. Not sure of his state of mind.

"Yes, I'm fine, nurse Jully," he replied somewhat irritated.

"I'm sorry," he apologized, "you mean well to ask. It's just that I had a rough night, you understand?"

"I understand Mr. Brannigan," she replied calm and perceptive. "It's only natural, considering the circumstances. I hope you feel better after having your breakfast and taking these." She handed him the small tablets and a glass of water.

"Yes, I hope so too," he replied, "I have a lot to organize today."

"Without a doubt," she said in acknowledgment. "If there's anything I can do to help, let me know," she added.

"Thank you, I appreciate that," he smiled somewhat.

When she had left, he searched for a funeral company. He wanted an elegant service for his Emily. Once he found one, he made a list of the people he wished to invite for the occasion.

He was glad that Emily's parents had already passed away. To tell parents that their daughter had committed suicide, let alone the reason, is the most dreadful thing to do! At least, he got spared that awful task.

He organized a Wake, for relatives and friends. And a small service, to honor Emily and her lifestyle. At which he said his final goodbye at the cemetery, with a personal poem.

Claire watched the black horse-drawn hearse. Two black funeral cars drove behind the carriage.

Even Matthew attended, in his own way.

A small group of people gathered around the grave. Claire found it difficult to withhold her weeping sounds. She hoped no one discovered her.

She saw Mason, all dressed in black, walking next to Leonardo. His head bowed towards the ground, his hands folded at the back, holding a small piece of paper.

After a few words by the pastor, he said his farewell. She got closer and she heard the words he spoke to his beloved Emily.

My darling Emily,
You were the light of my life,
and you were a caring wife.
Our love was not meant to last,
you ended your life, way too fast.
My darling, I will miss your warmth, your touch,
yes my darling, I will miss you so much.
I'm sorry you were not strong enough to see
how much you've always meant to me.
Rest in peace my darling Emily,
we'll meet again one day, you'll see.

Claire no longer watched the emotional scene that unfolded. Her back was aching because of the weight of the baby. When Mason finished reading, she made her way back to her car, moving slow and with care.

She sobbed, all the way back to the Monastery.

Chapter 24

During the months following Emily's funeral, Mason stayed at Chalton House during many weekends. To come to terms with the loss of his beloved wife. He welcomed the therapeutic sessions with Dr. Watson and Dr. Henry.
During one of his stay-overs, he received an unexpected message.
"Good morning, Mr. Brannigan!"
Nurse Jully walked into his room, cheerful and gloating. "I have a surprise for you!" She dangled a small package in front of him. "Delivered yesterday, late afternoon. Personal and confidential! I wonder why?"
With a teasing sparkle in her expecting eyes, she handed him the parcel. Wrapped in purple paper with a pink bow around it.
Mason looked in awe. Who sent him something? He didn't understand.
"Aren't you going to open it?"
Curious, the nurse waited in anticipation.
"There's no sender's address," she added. "Mysterious, don't you think?"
"Yes!" he replied, overpowered by this unexpected gift. He recognized a familiar scent when he opened the parcel.
"Oh! A diary!" The nurse giggled elated. "From a secret admirer?" She asked, straight forward.
Mason couldn't help but smile because of her extreme curiosity. It was none of her business and he wanted to send her away, to leave him alone. Yet, he didn't.
He turned the cover of the small diary with care.

And he recognized the curled handwriting.

"Dearest Mason,
My greatest wish is for us to be on speaking terms again. I heard the sad news about Emily and I send you my sincere condolences. This is my gift to you. And, although it may not erase the pain, I hope my writing will dissolve the sadness I have inflicted on you.
Yours always, Claire Attaway."

A chill ran down his spine. His breathing became heavier and his heartbeat increased. The effect annoyed him.
"And?" nurse Jully asked impatient, unaware of the turmoil inside his head.
"Read for yourself," he said, upset.
He returned the journal to her.
"How incredible!" she responded. "Wasn't she your first love, Mr. Brannigan?" Mason nodded in affirmation.
"You should read it, Mr. Brannigan!" She pushed the booklet in his hands. "To come to terms with the past," she suggested.
He stared at it for a while and placed it on the table near the window.
"Yes," he answered at long last, "perhaps I should."
Deep inside unconvinced. The memories painful and his heart ached! She ruined his marriage with Emily! And wanted him to read her life's story to make amends? What a nerve! She kept on haunting him, over and over again.
"Anyways, I leave you alone!" nurse Jully announced. "Have a nice day!"

He plumped down into his reading chair. Tapped with his fingers on the armrest and looked at Claire's diary again.

He smelled the wonderful and familiar perfume. The odor of delicate flowers she so often used to wear. A painful reminder of the romantic moments they shared.

How ironic she interfered with his muse over the past, the dead and the living! A hint of amusement glared in his eyes.

"She might even torment me in my sleep! To persuade me to read her memoirs," he envisaged, woeful.

"Fine!" he spoke out loud. "Have it your way, Claire Attaway!"

He took the diary from the table, returned to his chair and began to read.

"My dear Mason,

Here I am, spending a sabbatical year at the Healing Monastery in London. They welcomed me as a guest and forgave me my sins. Encouraged me to write my thoughts and experiences. Unload my past and heal the pain I caused to those around me. It sure helped me!

They sent this to you, in the hope you understand! To forgive me, so we all have peace, the rest of our lives.

Where to begin? The affair with Nathan?

That was a big mistake! As I told you. I caused both of us hurt and sadness. No matter how hard I tried, I never forgot you, Mason.

You loved and respected me. I should have treated you the same, you deserved it. You meant so much! I never intended to hurt Emily.

And I'm sorry I lured you back into my arms.
I had no right to do so. But, I could not help myself.
I'm not trying to make any excuses, but I had an inner urge to wind every man around my little finger. I needed the attention, to be admired. Not just by one man. No, by many! You may call it a mental illness. It's hard to believe, but please understand.
Although I looked self-assured, I wasn't. Deep inside, I wanted the affirmation I was attractive. I never realized that this personal need caused my despicable behavior.
At the Monastery, they opened my eyes!
By the time you read this, I am cured and I will make amends, my love. I hope you will too!"

Mason's eyes became watery when he finished her introduction. Well aware of Claire's urge to ensnare other men. It surprised him she herself perceived something was wrong. To stay at a Monastery, to find inner peace. And to apologize for her attitude.

"She must love me!" he thought, at a loss with this startling revelation. Not sure whether he should continue reading her diary or whether to put it aside. To let bygones be bygones.

He gazed out of the window. The branches of the trees waved in the wind. A blackbird tried to hold its grip but failed. It flew onto the grass and picked at whatever it found to eat.

I need to get a grip on my life and the emotions that go with it, Mason reflected melancholic. If I continue to read, I'll better understand Claire, to forget.

Now Emily is gone, it's perhaps time to overlook Claire's mistakes. To make allowances for the future! In case, she gives me reason enough to forgive her!

He went from page to page, pondering over her words. Her deepest fears and desires. The experiences in her youth and those in Australia with Nathan. That was the hardest part. Yet when he finished reading, he understood what happened. An emotional trauma for Claire.

With a loud and heavy sigh, he closed the booklet. This asked for serious consideration. He took a long walk along the countryside.

Chapter 25

Claire wrote her life story because Felipe urged her.
"Trust me, *Cara Mia*," he said, "it will help you heal!" And although reluctant to start, she was glad she did.
A long thin thread of enticement run through her complicated life. She needed to pull it out and replace it with a more sturdy material, Mason.
When Emily passed away that became a probability. And at last, Felipe agreed. He acknowledged it as the best solution for both of them. Thus, he suggested sending her diary to Mason. To make him sense their heartfelt entanglement.
But, Matthew interfered. He prepared himself and his mother for his birth. Claire experienced cramps and pains in her groin and lower back. Every joint and every muscle told her. Her little boy wanted to face the world. The contractions got stronger and more frequent.
She called Rose Blanchard, the midwife she had appointed.
"How often do you have the contractions?" Rose asked.
"Every five minutes," Claire's breathing became heavier.
"And, during a longer time? Say more than half an hour?"
"Yes, well, to me it's long!" Claire replied.
"All right, it might be time," Rose concluded.
"I will tell your physician and I'm on my way! Don't leave!"
"As if I can!" Claire considered, gasping for air due to another contraction. She tried to concentrate on her breathing, to stay calm.

It took ages before Rose arrived in her room at the Monastery.

The Abbey allowed her to give birth there and then since she had no complications during her pregnancy. They expected none. Claire was glad. She didn't want to go to a hospital.

"I miss you Mason!" she uttered, "at the birth of our son! Such a bonding, emotional experience for the three of us! Sorry that you're not here!"

Instead, Felipe and his wife Monica offered their emotional support. They had two children and experience with the procedures. Their presence comforted Claire. She needed their help more than ever!

When Rose arrived, she assessed Claire and took action.

"Yes, it's time!" she said. "Your son is due to arrive!"

She checked Claire's blood pressure, the baby's vital signs and more. But Claire didn't notice. The contractions came within seconds and frequent! She had to lie down in the position to give birth.

"Now," Rose spoke. "Try to follow your body's natural urges to push. When and if you are ready! In whatever way is right for you!"

Claire nodded her head.

Meanwhile, Monica and Felipe arrived. Monica held Claire's hand.

"You may squeeze it if you need to," she told Claire.

She accepted the invitation and hand-clasped her supporter firm at that point.

Then came the urge to push.

And she pushed! Again and again, until something popped out of her.

"The baby's head!" Rose announced. "Take another deep breath Claire and push, push. You can do it! Push!"

A loud scream came from her mouth when she gave the final thrust to bring Matthew into the world.

"Well done Mummy!" Rose saluted her. "Well done!"

She cut the cord and checked Matthew's vital signs. When he cried, everybody in the room cheered and applauded.

Except for Claire! She vomited! It splashed over her and she yelled in disgust.

"Oh! I'm so sorry! I didn't expect this!"

"That's all right dear," Rose comforted her. "It happens to the best of us. Nothing unusual. Let me help clean yourself."

When that was over and done with, Rose handed her son over to her.

Claire smiled at the little human in her arms. She took his tiny hands and held them soft and gentle with two fingers.

"Hello Matthew," she whispered. "It has been a tremendous journey for the both of us! But from now on, things will get better, I promise."

Two dark, familiar eyes looked at her in awe. Her son! Happy and relaxed.

"He's beautiful!" Monica said. "Congratulations Claire!"

"Yes, congratulations!" Felipe added.

"You have a handsome young man, whom I guess looks after his father?"

"Yes," Claire admitted, "he does!" Mason will be so proud once he gets to meet his son!"

Faithless Romance

A stream of motherly love embraced her.

The weeks after Matthew's arrival, Claire's paternal instincts took over.

She nursed him, fed him, and bathed him. Sang him to sleep, and adored everything about him. The way he smiled at her made her heart melt.

She learned to read his signals for needing his food or if his diaper needed changing. Monica visited them often. They took Matthew for a stroll in his pram if the weather permitted.

Claire wrote her emotions and her son's progress in a diary. In the back of her mind, she believed Mason returned in her life. And if he did, he'd want to read about Matthew's first months or years as a baby.

Even though her counseling sessions with Felipe ended, he still kept an eye on her. During one of his visits, he asked, "can I send your diary to Mason, Claire? Remember we talked about that?"

"Yes I do remember," she replied, with guilt. "I'm not sure. No time to reconsider, taking care of Matthew."

"I understand," he agreed, "but if you still wish to win Mason over, it's important he gets it."

He scanned her face with his eyes, trying to work out how she felt about it at this stage.

"Of course," she admitted. "In fact, I wish he saw his son and helped raise him. But I want him to come back because he loves me and misses me! Not because he is responsible and therefore takes care of his son."

She lowered her eyelids and Felipe responded with sympathy.

Faithless Romance

"Sure," he said, "that's how it should be!"

A short silence followed.

"If you write a small introduction to your diary," he then suggested, "I will make sure he gets it. Sprinkle that lovely perfume you wear onto the pages. It may bring back happy memories to him."

"What a wonderful idea!" she responded, grateful. "Thanks, Felipe, I'll never forget what you've done for me!"

He waved her remarks aside. "No need to thank me, Cara, it's only natural I help such an amazing woman like yourself. You've been through a lot and it's time you get the love you are longing for. Apart from the love that little Matthew is giving you," he added with a broad grin on his face.

She laughed sincerely. "Speaking of whom, he's awake!" She heard a soft chuckle coming from the cot.

"You can collect the diary tomorrow Felipe, I'll have it ready for you."

"Wonderful! Oh, and when are you moving out of the Monastery? You said something about buying a small house somewhere?"

"Next month," she replied, "around the 25th of May. I found this lovely cottage in Aylesbury, where Matthew can play in the garden."

"Good for you! Monica, me and the kids will soon come for a visit. We love the countryside!"

"That's a deal!" she smiled, meanwhile attending to Matthew, who needed a diaper change.

"Right, I will leave you to it then," he said, "good luck with that," he pointed at the dirty nappy.
"Thanks," she replied pulling a funny face, holding a finger against her nostrils. "By the smell of it, I'll need it!"
He giggled and left the room.

Mason returned from his long walk during which he searched his soul. Emily meant the world to him, but deep inside he never stopped loving Claire. His adoration genuine, from the moment he set eyes on her.
Yes, she hurt him, and she angered him! But he accepted her explanation. He understood why. The elopement and later her return shouldn't have surprised him.
What she wrote in her diary confirmed his perception. Still, when it happened he got hurt. He experienced a sense of great loss at the time. But he wanted to forget and forgive and move on.
With Emily gone and Claire now brought to her senses, he needed her more than ever. He wanted to believe that her stay at the Monastery and the counseling she received, changed her. Claire could give him the children he longed for.
Back at Chalton House, he packed up, ready to leave. To re-start his life and pay more attention to his now downsized business. With enough earnings to support a family.
That same evening he sat at the table in his own apartment, writing a letter to Claire, inviting her over for dinner, come what may.

Chapter 26

"Stuff it!" Nathan yelled when he left the conference room. "What's wrong with you people!" he shouted while he rushed through the office corridor. "I can't believe it!" He stormed into his own office at the end of the hall and shut the door behind him with a loud bang. Ignoring the advice of his anger management course.
He crashed down into his chair, threw his feet on the desk and folded his arms behind his head. Enraged, he grabbed a pen and paper.
"I'm handing in my resignation, as per today!" he said, angry and irritated. "That shows them who's in charge of my life!" he grumbled. "Idiots!" His fist hurt when he hit the desk with blunt force.
At that moment, the door swung wide open and Brian, one of the company directors, came charging in.
"Now, look here Nathan!" he began. "There's no need to make such a fuss! We appreciate your talents, but this is unacceptable. We're dealing with an important client here. Not just anybody! She won't accept it!"
"Well, you have a strange way of showing your appreciation!" Nathan responded still outraged.
"Once again, I worked late last evening. To get this advertisement ready for this jewelry stuff! You wiped it off the table as pure nonsense! Respect goes a long way! I don't deserve this Brian!"
Nathan paced up and down the room when he continued.
"I spent many evenings with this firm, instead of enjoying myself."

Faithless Romance 135

He lied! He thought of the passionate nights with this client. Nights that triggered memories of other intense moments. Moments he used to share with Claire Attaway.

"This advertisement will work!" he argued. "I'm a hundred percent convinced! Since when do you not value my gut feeling Brian?"

"Because, Nathan, she will not accept your idea!"

A soft moan sounded from Nathan's lips. He gazed at the high rises of Sydney, through the window of his elevated office.

If anyone knows the client well, it's me, he thought. If only Brian knew how well I know their client! Then we wouldn't have this argument right now!

But company policy didn't allow for any personal relationships with clients. There was no way he'd mention that!

Brian looked sour when he turned to face him. "I'm sorry Nathan," he said. "Will you give it another chance and re-think before tomorrow?"

"Yes, Brian! One more evening for the firm won't hurt me!" Nathan sneered and grinned.

"Fine, that's settled then." Brian left the room, satisfied.

Nathan waited until the director was out of sight. He then took his stuff out of his desk and threw it into a box.

He left his resignation letter for everyone to see and he shut the door behind him.

"I said it earlier and I say it again! As of now, I am taking charge of my life!" He left the building. Back in control.

He couldn't wait to see their faces!

Once they found out he was the new advertising director of the Splendor Jewelry line! He would persuade Julia to give him the job. And even better, it meant a return to London!

He wished to renew his affair with Claire. His new boss lady wouldn't be around that much and his top job might impress Claire! Enough to have a fling or two, to meet his needs.

Claire looked around her fabulous new home. The surroundings were stunning! Close to a historic town, with ancient streets, riverside walks, and famous markets.

The cottage had a large, picturesque flower garden and grass for Matthew to play on. Inside were three bedrooms, a living and dining room, kitchen and bathroom. When you entered the house, the main bedroom was on the right. Not only the perfect location to live for her and her son! She found the perfect nanny to enable her to go back to work part-time.

But most important, she received a letter from Mason! A few weeks earlier, in which he invited her for a meal at his place, in two weeks time.

"I'm off to work now Macy!" she yelled out at her child carer, who was busy with Matthew in his own, bright blue bedroom. She gave him a hug and a kiss earlier on, to say goodbye. Afraid of her own emotions in front of Macy.

"Okay, Miss Attaway! Have a nice day!" the girl shouted in return.

Although confident the 19-year-old Macy took good care of her Matthew, she found it difficult to let go.

Yet, she needed to work. Not only for the money!

She wanted to swap changing nappies for more mind bugling challenges. An encounter with Nathan Kingsley, though, wasn't one of them!

It struck as a lightning bolt on a cloudless day! An absolute horror scenario that frightened her to death when it unfolded.

"Claire, do you have a minute?" her boss Jim Moore, walked into her office.

"Sure Jim, what can I do for you?" she responded, meanwhile looking up from her computer screen. She stretched her back, waiting for his answer.

"It's great to have you with us," he started. "We acquired a big account, Splendor Jewelry. The owner and director Julia Splendor asked us to set up a marketing campaign. Together with her new advertising director. I asked him to come in today and he arrived." He paused and looked at her with enthusiasm.

"I realize you started today! But, it is the right account for you to handle. Because of your earlier experience with a jewelry line, and your excellent marketing skills."

"That sounds interesting," she said. "I'm available."

"Great! I'll ask him to come in," Jim walked out to return seconds later.

"Claire, may I introduce you to the advertising director of Splendid Jewelry!"

She froze solid, unable to move, nor to speak.

This can't be real! She choked. I'm having a nightmare!

"Hello, Claire!"

She recognized the voice and two familiar bright blue eyes stared at her. They belonged to a Greek god who once conquered her. Now he caused an enormous electric shock-wave, going through her entire body.
Unaware of her inner turmoil, Jim smiled content.
"Ah! You two are acquainted? That's even better! I leave you both alone. Good luck!" And off he went.
He left Claire with the remnants of an unpleasant past. Disabled and vulnerable.

Chapter 27

"Aren't you going to shake my hand?" Nathan asked with an arrogant look on his face. "After all, I'm a respected customer!"

Claire managed to get a grip on her emotions and she rose from her chair. She moved around her desk and strode toward him. Her eyes shot fire and she boiled inside.

"How dare you!" She lashed out at him. "How dare you turn up in London, at my company! Haven't you done enough!" She stamped the floor with her feet, like a frustrated horse. She wanted to slap him in the face, but she knew she couldn't.

"You have to be my client?!" She fired back at him. "Not in a million years! I will explain it to Jim, he'll understand. He can assign someone else to do the job!"

"Oh! Come on, Claire! Don't be a spoilsport! You are the best in your field. You know it, I know it and your boss knows it! You can't let a personal feud interfere with your work! How unprofessional!"

He challenged her, his blue pupils became even brighter. He looked her straight in the eyes. He wasn't going to back down and Claire sensed it.

She looked him up and down. She couldn't help it, he looked stunning in his gray suit. This time, though, she observed, without feeling an immediate sexual attraction. She learned her lesson and Nathan needed one, she concluded.

"Fine!" she replied, still angry with him, "you want professionalism, you get it! Take a seat, Mr. Kingsley."

She pulled a chair over for him. He grinned and looked defiant. He tried to touch her in the process, but she made sure he couldn't.

"Alright, alright!" He gave in. "Have it your way, for now!" he added. "After all, I do have my obligations as well! Otherwise, Julia will take revenge."

"I'm glad to see you are afraid of someone," Claire derived.

"Afraid is an overstatement," he replied with a broad smile on his face. "Let's say she can be demanding and she has a strange way of showing that, sexually, if you know what I mean."

Claire frowned her dark eyebrows. "No, I don't know what you mean," she responded, agitated. "And I don't want to know it either." She shivered. Whatever went on between Julia and Nathan, it was not only professional she thought. "Who knows what those two do in their spare time." She couldn't even begin to imagine.

"How's Mason?" he asked, catching her by surprise.

"Great," she said, "not that it's any of your business." She knew her cheeks colored red at that point.

"Ah!' he noticed, "you're back together, how sweet!"

"No, we're not!" she denied, immediately regretting it. Because it might be in her favor if he thought she was.

"What a fool!" he responded.

"And why exactly?" she asked, offended.

"That's obvious, isn't it? No man in his right mind would let a gorgeous woman like you slip away!"

"Ha! Look who's talking!" she argued.

Faithless Romance

"I think we can both agree that you could not hold on to me either?"

"Whatever gave you that idea?" He now got agitated. "You were the one that threw me out the door, remember?"

"Yes, and why do you think that was, remember?" she provoked him. "Thank God it turned out I wasn't pregnant at the time!"

"Pregnant?" He looked at her with widened eyes, flabbergasted. "We always used protection!"

"Not when you decided to rape me!"

Touche! He flinched.

"That never was my intention. I …."

"Stop Nathan, enough!" Claire was adamant. "No more talk about our past. I have a son, but he's Mason's and I am so happy about that!"

"And he doesn't know, I gather?"

"No, not yet, but he soon finds out."

"How?"

"I will tell him, of course."

"Mmmmm."

"Now, what's this company you are representing, Splendor Jewelry? We do need to get down to business, Nathan!"

"Fine, we'll continue this conversation later on."

"I doubt it," she replied firm and resolute.

He kept silent. He took several documents out of his briefcase and began to introduce her to his firm.

When he finished his presentation, Claire felt uneasy. Splendor Jewelry sounded interesting enough as a company to do marketing for.

But it also felt as a betrayal towards Mason.

After all, if she and Mason became a couple again, his jewelry chain of stores meant their future. It wouldn't be right to start promoting another, similar business.

"Look, Nathan," she said. "What you just told me is most interesting and it will always stay within these four walls. But you have to understand that I cannot accept this project."

"And why not?" he asked insulted and suspicious.

She sighed, despondent.

"No, wait! I think I begin to understand," he derived from her posture. "It's Mason, isn't it? You don't feel comfortable with me nor the project, because of him!" He leaned backward in his chair, frowning his eyebrows.

"You must appreciate that Nathan!" she responded irritated. "You should realize that Julia is not going to be too happy when she finds out about us! And more so about me and my connection to Mason's business!" She knew she hit the right button.

He became restless and his eyes wandered towards the windows.

"Julia! Yes, that's a good point," he admitted. "Why didn't I think of that?"

"Because, as usual, you only thought about yourself and your wish to put me on the spot. That's why!" She sneered at him.

"Calm down Claire, there's no need to be so angry! I underestimated the situation, that's all."

He shoved the paperwork back into his case and got out of his chair.

"It's obvious you've chosen for Mason. I hope he doesn't disappoint you again!" He tried to undermine her confidence.

"I'm sure he won't," she replied. "Besides, that's none of your business." She sensed that her own negative feelings towards the man in front of her took a hold of her. How arrogant of him to say that.

"I think you better leave," she told him in a vigorous manner. "I will inform Jim about our conflict of interest. I'm sure he will appreciate my sensitivity. And I'm also convinced he'll find someone else within our firm to work with you and Julia."

"As you wish," he sighed, disappointed. "I thought you'd grab this opportunity with both hands, Claire. I'm sorry for your stubbornness."

He walked towards the door and turned around.

"You will regret this," he exclaimed, "you will!"

"If you say so Nathan," she replied, fed up with his behavior. "Close the door behind you please."

She turned her computer on and pretended to read something important. She avoided any further eye contact with him.

When she, at last, heard the door slam behind him, she allowed herself to take a breather. She hoped she never saw him again.

She gave Macy a call to see whether everything was fine with her and Matthew. Nathan soon disappeared to the background.

Chapter 28

Claire never imagined Nathan dared to return to London. And she never dreamed he had the guts to visit her at her office. How he found out where she worked remained a mystery.

She watched the city from her desk. The place where she found love and then lost it, due to her own stupid mistakes. But then recovered from her misjudgment and the grief it caused. She wanted a more fulfilling life, stable and secure.

Her wounds healed, but Nathan re-opened them.

Why? she thought, troubled. Why can't he leave me alone?

She bit her lower lip out of frustration and anger. What did he mean by saying I'll regret this? Is it a real threat or just a remark to taunt me? A question not easy to answer.

Nathan proved unpredictable.

When the letter arrived at her home, three days later, she found out what it meant. He demanded a DNA test to confirm whether he fathered her son or not. She stared at the piece of paper in front of her and called her sister.

"The arrogance! To ask for proof! It's obvious it can't be his!" She flared up. "What's wrong with him? He can't be serious, Caro! He's crazy!"

"Yes, he is," her sister replied. "But as long as you're certain, nothing can go wrong! There's nothing to fear!"

"I am!" Claire answered agitated. "Nathan and I were separated for over a month before I caught up with Mason."

"I see," her sister commented, keeping silent for a moment before responding.

"The DNA test will show Nathan he's wrong. Sounds good to me."

"I guess so," Claire admitted. "Let's hope Nathan then disappears and stays out of my life!"

"Yes, I hope he does," Caroline agreed. "That's best for everyone! What day do you go?"

"Next week, the 14th. I'll text you the outcome. I don't know when the results are in. I'll ask them."

"I wish you the best of luck, Sis. Try not to worry! Talk to you later. Time for me to prepare dinner. Take care!"

"Thanks, Caro, you too! Bye! Enjoy your meal!"

Claire switched off her phone, drained. She never asked for this to happen! And she never expected this!

Caroline confirmed her own thoughts.

She hung the letter on her fridge. Underneath a Kangaroo magnet, she brought along from Australia.

The irony! she thought. She highlighted the date with a yellow marker to remind herself.

A noise on the footpath announced Macy's return from a walk in the park with Matthew.

"We had such a lovely walk, didn't we, Matthew?" Macy greeted her. "But I have to go home, my little fellow! To my Mummy."

"Thanks, Macy," Claire smiled at the young girl, "you're a star!"

"It's my pleasure Mrs. A! Matthew is a real happy boy. He smiles and smiles at everyone and everything."

Faithless Romance

She grabbed her stuff from the sofa.

"See you again tomorrow Mrs. A! Bye, Matthew, bye!" She waved one more time before she disappeared from sight.

Claire devoted the rest of the day to her son. Nathan disappeared to the background, and no longer occupied her mind.

During the evening, when Matthew lay asleep in his own room, she looked at the dreaded letter on the fridge. Her heart palpitated and her body-heat shot up.

You will pay the price for this sleazy action, Nathan! She contemplated revenge. I won't let you get away with this! It's time for a heart to heart talk with your employer, Julia. Being a woman herself, she may sympathize with me. I hope I can persuade her to send you back to Australia, to handle her affairs over there!

She pictured his departure, and it brought a grin to her face. "Yes, a good idea," she mumbled.

She slept like a rose that night. Refreshed, she woke up.

The sun's rays played with items in her room and cast weird and funny shadows on her bedroom wall.

Matthew slept through the night with no disturbances. She looked in on him and he gave her a welcoming smile when she entered his room.

"Hello, darling!" she said when she picked him up. "You're a good boy! Mummy will change your nappy and then we share breakfast together! Before Macy gets here."

She caressed his cheek with her fingers and brushed through the thin hairs on his head. She took him outside for their early morning meal.

There was no wind and plenty of sunshine.

The morning paper lay waiting for her on the lawn. She enjoyed a black cup of coffee and the laughter of Matthew. He pointed at the birds in the garden, having fun.

She flipped through the daily review until her gaze fell on an article with a familiar name and photo! Her eyes widened and her mouth opened in awe! She read the interview with Nathan, in his role as Marketing and Advertising Director of Splendor Jewelry.

To her disgust, he mentioned Mason's store chain. He called it outdated, and his merchandise too expensive. He even suggested that his company considered taking over Brannigan's! How dare he!

She ripped the story out of the page, folded the journal and slammed it onto the table. Matthew looked at her with scared eyes.

"Sorry darling, Mummy is upset," she spoke to him in a soft tone. She tried to divert his attention by showing him his favorite toy, a small, white fluffy rabbit.

To her relief, it worked, and he soon forgot the issue.

She looked at her watch. Five minutes to eight! Macy will arrive any minute now! I can't wait to get to my office to begin my crusade against Nathan. What if Mason reads the article? she thought, then he knows Nathan is back in London! It revives the hurt and the anger. He might consider canceling our dinner date! I have to take action! I can't allow that to happen!

Just then, Macy walked through the gate. "Good morning, Mrs. A.!" she called out cheerful and smiling.

"What a gorgeous day it is today! Hello, Matthew! How are you, little boy?"

She took his tiny hand and gave him a tender kiss. He giggled, and it was obvious he adored his nanny.

After her daily briefing with Macy, Claire took off. The traffic flowed well towards the city this morning and within half an hour she sat at her desk. She grabbed the phone and dialed the number of Splendor Jewelry.

"Good morning, my name is Claire Attaway, the Corporate Account Manager at Baxter Management. I'd like to speak with Mrs. Julia Splendor, please? It is rather urgent!"

"One moment," the receptionist answered, "I'll put you through."

Claire hoped she wouldn't get Nathan instead. She relaxed when her call got through.

"Good morning, this is Julia. What can I do for you, Miss Attaway?"

Claire explained why she contacted her and she tried to be quick and brief. She wanted Julia on her side. She had to understand! After her summary of events, Julia remained silent for a while. Claire heard her breathe. The news astounded her.

"Well, what can I say?" she said. "Those are serious allegations. I suggest we meet for lunch, to discuss it in more detail. I can't make it today.

Does tomorrow suit you?"

"Yes, that's fine!" Claire responded. "I realize it's a complicated situation. I agree we better talk it over in person. Around one tomorrow? At Debenhams?"

"Yes, that sounds good," Julia confirmed. "Until then!"
"Until tomorrow," Claire ended the call.
She heaved a deep sigh, grateful that Julia seemed prepared to listen. "We'll see who has the last laugh, Nathan!" she murmured, "we'll see!"
Another call, this time from a client, asked her attention.
She soon got back into her normal daily office routine.
Mason read the news in the paper, again and again.
First with disbelief, then getting upset. Angry as hell! This charlatan dared to speak about his business! And since when was he back in London? Did Claire know of his return? Did she keep this from him? Could he trust her? Or would she betray him once more? Mind boggling questions, to which he needed an answer.

Chapter 29

When Julia Splendor entered a room, people turned their heads. Her eccentric looks attracted attention. She wore several diamond rings. One on every finger. Extravagant, braided necklaces accentuated a bright colored red and blue dress. To cover up her voluptuous figure.
Claire couldn't imagine what Nathan saw in her. But then again, he always displayed unexpected character traits.
"I'm so glad you agreed to meet me," she welcomed Julia to her table at the restaurant. "Even though your time is valuable!"
"Don't mention it!" the female executive replied. "If I can help another woman in need, I'm more than happy to oblige!" She observed her surroundings. Then returned her gaze to Claire. "You are a stunning woman!" she commented. "Nathan has a taste for beauty and excellence!"
Deep inside, Claire suppressed a giggle after this remark. Seeing Julia's own disposition.
"Let's get to the point!" Julia offered. "There's no time like the present!" Meanwhile, she looked over the menu. She asked Claire for her choice and ordered their luncheon.
"Right, here we go," Claire announced.
She explained her past ordeal with Nathan. And her connection with Mason Brannigan. Julie listened without interfering. Claire finished and expressed her discontent with the recent article in the paper.
"What do you want from me?" Julia asked.

Faithless Romance

"Well," Claire suggested. "Can you ask for a rectification? Explain that your Marketing Executive got things out of proportion."

She watched Julia's facial expression. Yet she showed no emotion or anger.

"You do realize what you ask of me?" she responded at last. "What can you offer me in return?"

"What do you have in mind?" Claire asked.

"It could help if you take up the marketing campaign for our company again. I will appoint another person to work with you, of course!" she added with a smirk on her face.

Claire wavered to accept. Yet she knew her client's worth. She had to make it work!

"In that case," she said, "I'd be happy to!"

"Then that's settled!" Julia concluded. "Thanks for this inspiring intermezzo and the helpful information, Claire." She got up to leave. "I'm sure we will be in touch again soon."

"Thank you too! Julia! I do appreciate your consideration and efforts. You won't regret it!" Claire said as she walked towards the exit alongside her.

Once Julia had gone out of sight, she relaxed. That went well! A subtle revenge! Now all that remained was the result of the DNA test. If that gave the desired result, her future with Mason was secured. At that moment, her cell phone rang.

She recognized Mason's voice.

"Mason! How good to hear from you! You were just on my mind!"

Faithless Romance

"Did you see the article in yesterday's paper?"
He got straight to the point.
"Your ex-boyfriend is back in town and up to his old tricks!"
"Yes," she responded. "I read it and it left me aghast! End of last week, I found out he returned from Australia. This is unbelievable!"
"So before that, you didn't know he returned?" he inquired.
"No! I did not!" she reacted, annoyed. "I'd never hide the truth from you anymore, Mason!" she said with a firm tone in her voice. "Trust me!" She became emotional. Nathan almost succeeded to ruin her renewed relationship with Mason. She couldn't let that happen!
"Please, Mason! I will explain everything to you next week. And I promise you, I took revenge for his latest action. He's not getting away with it. Your company will get saved and reinstated. It is my personal quest to make that happen!" She sounded convincing and determined. And she meant it.
"Good!" Mason responded, satisfied. "I'm glad you're frank and that you mean business. Shall I respond with an open letter to the paper?"
"No, leave it, Mason! I have my connections. I'm going to rectify the matter!"
"Great! I look forward to seeing you again. Take care!"
"Same to you, Mason. Don't worry!"

Chapter 30

A week later, Mason sets the table with his best dishes.
Anxious to see Claire and uncertain about the revival of their relationship. They both went through traumatic experiences.
Circumstances changed and they both learned from their slip-ups, which benefited their future together.
He wished to attempt, to try again. If it went well, he planned to invite her for a long weekend trip.
To stay at the Ardtara Country House in Upperlands, Northern Island. An elegant and restored 19th-century mansion. Between Belfast and the Giant's Causeway Coast, hidden away in the rolling hills.
But first, there was tonight. He couldn't call himself a master chef in cooking. Yet he prepared a three-course meal for their first make-it-up rendezvous. As a starter, a pear salad, with goat cheese and walnuts.
The main course was chicken filet with apples and small onions. Served with small Parisian potatoes on the side. As a dessert, he chose a soft chocolate mousse with whipped cream. He selected a Lafayette Empire Bordeaux Exquisite wine to celebrate the occasion. The tone set for a pleasant evening.
Time to change into light beige trousers and a green and white striped blouse with short sleeves. It had been a warm day. He opened the doors to his balcony and took in the view and the balmy evening air. His apartment bordered a small park.

Faithless Romance

Nearby stood several mature birch trees, giving shade from the sun during the hot summer days.
Then the doorbell rang to announce Claire's arrival.
Apprehensive, he opened the door. His doubts faded away. She looked even more beautiful than he remembered.
Her auburn hair fell in layers around her almond colored face. And her mouth curved into an incredible smile. A soft yellow dress with tiny blue butterflies followed the curves of her slender figure.
When he laid eyes on her, his heart rate increased. He made the right decision to ask her over.
"Hello Mason!" she said, with a radiant smile. "Thank you for inviting me! It's been a long time!"
"Hello Claire!" he responded, pleased and cheerful. "You look amazing! Come in! I'm glad you're here."
To her disappointment, they kissed quick and polite. She understood his hesitation. Rushing things might spoil it.
"I see you still have that great view from your balcony," she said, stepping outside. "Isn't it a lovely evening?"
He joined her, and his body heat radiated. His aftershave triggered her senses.
"It's as if I've never been away," she whispered.
To her relief and delight, he agreed. "Yes, it is!"
For a moment she thought he wanted to touch her hand, but he didn't.
"Come, let's eat first, otherwise, I'm afraid the food won't taste that great anymore," he said. "Can I pour you a Bordeaux wine?"
"Yes, please, thank you. That's a fantastic wine! A good choice!"

Faithless Romance

"I knew you'd appreciate it," he grinned, "you always had a liking for exquisite drinks." He heaved his glass.

"To us," he said and clinked the glasses. "And a new beginning!"

"Yes, a new beginning," she repeated. Ecstatic about his obvious consent to their renewed kinship. No need to talk things through. They did right. It clicked straight away.

My personal diary helped him to forgive, she thought. Grateful that Felipe insisted she sent it.

When Mason presented her with the food, she complimented him.

"You learned how to cook!" she said, "it's delicious Mason!"

"I'm glad you enjoy it," he replied, charmed.

"How are you?" he then asked. "Still at the Monastery?"

"Oh no!" she replied enthusiastically. "I've moved to a lovely cottage in Aylesbury. Wait till you see it! You'll fall in love with it too!"

"Aylesbury? An amazing part of the countryside! Not far from London. A good idea," he admitted.

"You still work for the same company?"

"Yes, I was lucky to get the transfer back from Sydney," she answered. "And they allowed me to have a sabbatical. I couldn't ask for a better employer."

"Right," he said. He took a sip of his wine and continued.

"I have downsized the business. I needed more time for myself, to work things out," he paused. "And I want to spend more time with you if you allow me?"

He looked at her, his eyes dark and intense, waiting for her to respond.

Faithless Romance

"That's wonderful Mason!" she replied gleefully, "I'd love that!"
"So do I," he became flustered. He took her hands and caressed them before he asked the question.
"Will you join me for a long weekend to a romantic country house in Northern Ireland?" he asked.
"I will!" she said, grateful and excited. "But, there's something I need to tell you first!" she began.

Chapter 31

He pulled his hands away from her. She noticed his uneasiness at her announcement.

"Don't be alarmed, Mason!" she added. "My news will make you happy!"

"I hope so Claire. No bad news for me, please! I can't handle any more!" He looked sad and angry.

"Oh, Mason, I'm sorry! I didn't want to frighten or upset you! Let's be happy! This is a blessing for both of us!"

She had to admit she became nervous for his reaction.

"You see, the last time we said goodbye, I found out that I was pregnant! And meanwhile I have given birth to a son, our son Mason! His name is Matthew!"

She held her breath, waiting for a possible outburst.

"A son?" he responded at last, in total disbelief. "A son? Are you sure it is mine?"

"Yes!" she answered self-assured. "There's no doubt about that!"

"But how, when?"

"We may have been careless when we met in the motels, upon my return from Australia," she confessed. "We were in such a euphoric state!"

"Yes, of course! You're right!" For a second, he felt a painful stab in his heart. He remembered the day he found Emily in bloody water in the bathroom. But he forced himself to shut the door on those awful memories.

Claire saw his inner turmoil on his face and she understood his predicament.

Faithless Romance

"Don't worry, a DNA test confirmed that he is your son! We can be a family together," she said.

"And we can have another child," she added. "We are both ready for this. You can live with us in the cottage. It has a wonderful garden!"

She walked up to him and he pulled her on his lap.

"You still know how to seduce a man, Claire!" he laughed a happy laugh. "Even if you are a mother!" he smiled. "Who would have ever thought this? This is the most fantastic news I received in a long time! Matthew! You named him after my late father!"

He held her close to his breast. She heard his heart beating strong and loud. She looked up at him and kissed him on the mouth, soft and gentle. He responded at once.

For the first time in her life, Claire got the happy ending she wished for.

Mason visited Matthew during the next four weeks. He surrendered to their shared happiness. His son meant the world to him. And Matthew adored his father.

A month later, he asked Claire to marry him. This time, they'd have a proper wedding!

She called her sister Caroline in Spain to share the big news.

"Caro, it's me, Claire! I think I'm getting married!"

"You what? You think? What do you mean?" her sister responded, giggling. "You either get married or you don't. Do I know him?"

"Yes, you do. I met him a long time ago when I bumped into him on the street, remember?!"

"Mason?" her sister asked in disbelief. "Are you sure?!"

"Yes! I am as certain as I will ever be! It's for real!" Claire tried to explain. She wished Caroline confirmed to her it was the right thing to do.

"Do you still love him? Are you ready?" Caroline asked.

"I do!" she responded. "No more fear for commitment. I'm ready! Matthew will have a real family!"

"Ah! Thank goodness for that! Claire, getting married is not an imprisonment! Besides, you can always walk out again if it isn't what you expected it to be!"

"That wouldn't be fair to Mason, nor to Matthew. He loves me with heart and soul! I don't want to delude him, not again!"

"Then there's nothing to worry about, is there?" Caroline answered with her usual common sense. "Seems to me you should marry him."

"Yes," Claire responded. "Can you come over and stay with me? I planned on asking you to be the maid of honor, anyway. I do depend on your ongoing support."

"Of course! I can!" she responded. "Let me take care of a few things over here. I'll be with you next week. How does that sound?"

"Wonderful! Thanks, Sis, you're the best!"

"That's what sisters are for! Don't over-think this marriage thing Claire. If it feels good, it is good. You're not getting any younger. Give it a go!"

With that solid advice, their phone conversation ended. Claire was happy her sister came over from Spain.

After the tragic death of their parents, she was the only close family member left.

Lucky for them, they got along fine now.

Faithless Romance

They chose an 18th Century Palladian Mansion as the venue for their wedding. Licensed for civil ceremonies.

It had vast acres of parkland, reception rooms, and luxury bedroom suites. Only a forty-minute drive from London.

There would be a small gathering of people. They invited their closest relatives and friends. Around forty guests.

Mason had no brothers or sisters, and his parents had already passed away. So he asked his longtime friend Leonardo Stevens to be his best man.

Caroline was Claire's maid of honor. And she had two more bridesmaids, being her closest friends.

The color scheme they had chosen was a dark blue for the men and a soft lilac for the bridesmaid. Claire's wedding dress remained a secret.

After a hectic number of days, preparing their wedding, the actual day arrived.

Is it really happening? She thought. What if I panic and walk out on him at the last minute? She trembled and looked uncomfortable.

Mason felt just as nervous. He paced up and down his apartment, meanwhile trying to get dressed for the occasion.

A knock on the door demanded his attention. When he opened it, Leonardo stood smiling before him.

"Mason, my good fellow, how are things? Are you ready to tie the knot for the second time?"

He responded with a wry face.

"I guess so," he said, somberly. "Let's hope Claire is too!"

"Cheer up man! Don't be anxious! It will be fine, you'll see!

She's a lucky girl to get you and I'm sure she's aware of that my friend!"
But Mason's confidence faltered.

Chapter 32

He questioned Claire's steadfastness. What if she changed her mind at the last minute? He just wished this part could be over and done with, to give him a sense of security and belonging. He admitted that her eternal loyalty towards him and therefore his marriage, remained fragile. But he couldn't let her slip away again. Not this time!
"Well, let's go!" Leonardo urged him. "We don't want to be late, do we?"
In a white Mercedes Benz, hired for the day, they drove to Claire's apartment to pick her up. Her sister opened the door and she was full of enthusiasm and excitement.
"She looks so amazing Mason!" she spilled the beans, meanwhile walking into the living room with him.
And there she was! The woman of his dreams, standing in the middle of the room. Looking like a princess who just stepped out of a fairy tale.
The dress a sparkling white with long fitted sleeves.
A full-length ball gown. A silhouette of layered satin with floral embroidery and crystal beading. A beautiful waste line and an amazing train behind it. Her hair braided with shiny pearls. Mason took it all in, blown away and speechless.
She smiled at him with the whole expression of her face. Radiant with happiness and tenderness.
Any doubts he still might have had evaporated into thin air.
"You are the most beautiful woman in the world!" he spoke with tears welling up in his eyes.

"You don't look so bad yourself," she replied, trying to joke around and with a teasing glint in her pupils.

She offered him her hand and he took it. He led her through the building, to the car. He couldn't take his eyes away from her. She knew he doted on her and he would give her anything she wanted.

But when they arrived at the venue she lost control of herself. She wanted to flee, to get out of there, to escape from it all.

"Claire and I will retreat into the back room," Caroline announced, sensing Claire's inner struggle. "We will rejoin you later on, for the vows."

She looked at a disturbed Mason. "Don't worry, she'll be there. Go on, you lot, go inside. The bride needs some space!"

Before Claire knew what happened, Caroline took her sister for a brisk walk to the right wing of the Mansion.

"You're having doubts again, haven't you?" she asked once they were inside.

"Was it that obvious?" Claire replied, walking up and down nervous and upset.

"To me, it was," Caroline answered. "I'm your sister, I sense those things right away!" She hugged her.

"Don't worry, it's only natural, especially for you," she added.

"You have a problem with tying yourself down. It surprised me when you called me and said you were getting married! But he's gorgeous Claire and he adores you!

Besides, he'll give you financial security, what more do you want?" She now looked firm and determined.
"You're getting married today, point. And anyway, you can always get a divorce if it turns out to be dreadful later on. Isn't it? I mean, you left him before, for that reason."
"I guess you are right, Caro!" Claire admitted, "I shouldn't worry about what could or could not happen right now.
And I have to do this, for Matthew! Thanks for being such an understanding sister." She kissed her on the cheek.
"I'm such a chicken sometimes. Like you said, it's time to grow up and get real!" She sighed. "Right, I'm ready! Now, let's go!"
Upon those words, the door burst open and Nathan crashed in. He wobbled unstable and intoxicated.
"There you are!" he spoke with a double tongue. "I must say, you look amazing! White becomes you Claire. Congratulations by the way, or perhaps not?" He laughed his head off.
The two women recovered from the initial shock wave.
"Nathan!?" Claire yelled with a high pitched voice. "How did you find us here? And why do you again behave so rude and unreasonable!" She gave him her most angry glare.
He roared and shuffled towards her. "I kept my eyes open, that's how." At that point, he almost fell over, against her precious dress. Caroline managed to interfere before he damaged or spoiled the delicate fabric.
"Out!" she shouted. "Get out of here, now!" She pushed him back through the door. "And don't think about joining the wedding crowd.

Faithless Romance

There will be serious consequences if you do!" She shut the door behind him with a loud bang.

"What an asshole!" Caroline said. "How dare he do this to you! Are you alright?"

"Yes, sort of, I think," Claire responded, shivering. "Is he gone yet? Otherwise, we are going to be late!"

Her sister looked through the window to see whether Nathan left.

"No sign of him," she replied. "Let's go!"

Somewhat flustered they arrived at the main venue. Both of them not mentioning a word about the brief episode.

"Are we still good?" Mason asked.

"Of course we are!" she replied. "I just had to rearrange something." She winked at him.

She turned around and smiled at Matthew. He lay on a friend's arm, quiet and content.

After a wonderful, romantic wedding ceremony, the marriage celebrant pronounced them husband and wife.

"You may now kiss the bride," he said. Claire's heart melted from the heat of his lips.

The Brannigan-Attaway family was re-born! No one destroyed that ever again! Not even a Nathan Kingsley!

Printed in Great Britain
by Amazon